In Crocodile Country

In Crocodile Country

Lalita Das

NIYOGI
BOOKS

Published by

NIYOGI BOOKS

D-78, Okhla Industrial Area, Phase-I
New Delhi-110 020, INDIA
Tel: 91-11-26816301, 49327000
Fax: 91-11-26810483, 26813830
email: niyogibooks@gmail.com
website: www.niyogibooks.com

Text©: Lalita Das
Editor: Gita Rajan
Cover Design: Write Media
Layout: Shashi Bhushan Prasad / Niyogi Books

ISBN: 978-93-81523-60-5
Publication: 2013

Printed at: Niyogi Offset Pvt. Ltd., New Delhi, India

This book is dedicated to all those who have
read and appreciated my first book
'Dancing with Kali'

Stage

*L*ounge of a resort somewhere along the Maharashtra-Gujarat highway.

Archways in the centres of left and right sides of stage leading to unseen spaces beyond. A small doorway is located in the left corner of the rear wall of the stage.

A narrow stairway starts from the archway at right and leads to a landing about one metre above the stage floor in the rear right corner of the stage. On the landing, an archway on the right leads to an unseen space beyond.

A small retractable balcony with two footlights in two corners in front is located high in the centre of the back wall. The balcony has side railings but is open in front. It is extended only during the blackout before a monologue and retracted during the blackout after it.

Two large windows are located in the rear wall between the rear door on the left and the stairs on the right and a small square window is located beside the archway on the left.

On the stage there are a sofa and a sofa chair strewn with throw cushions with colourful covers, a couple of straight-back hard chairs, a sideboard and a TV in the front with its back to the audience.

A few cheap throw rugs are thrown haphazardly on the floor.

There are colourful paintings on the walls, a plastic chandelier hanging in the middle, curios and knickknacks on the sideboard – all large, gaudy and cheap.

Overall effect is of cheap clutter.

A large grandfather clock ticks on the rear wall below the retractable balcony in the centre of the two windows.

Characters

Mathew: Portly man in early 40s, dressed in a dark
                     suit. Has fawning manners.

Vikram & Reema: Very rich and high society handsome couple.
                     Vikram is in late 30s, Reema in early 30s,
                     both dressed expensively in casual slacks
                     and shirt / top, silk scarves. Both display
                     arrogance of their class.

Salim: Slim, good looking, clean shaven, in early
                     30s, dressed casually yet artistically in slacks
                     and shirt with a scarf around his neck. Moves
                     like a cat and is alert and coiled up even
                     when seemingly relaxed.

Jai: Slim with a close-cropped beard, in early
                     30s, with the air of an intellectual, dressed in
                     kurta-pyjama.

Shanaz: Cheaply attractive, sexy, in late 20s,
                     dressed in a cheap salwar-kameez and
                     a dupatta.

Rajesh: Lower middle class, in early 20s, wearing synthetic trousers and shirt. Has cowardly, retreating manners.

Security guard:	Athletic, alert, dressed in black, carrying a gun.
Deviji:	In her 50s, dressed in a white cotton sari with a broad border, with mannerisms that are simultaneously arrogant and falsely humble.
Secretary:	Efficient looking, in his 40s, obsequious, dressed in a safari suit.
Priest:	Stooping old Christian man of Church dressed in a black robe. Displays both humility and strength of his faith.

Time Period

Whole action takes place during a few hours of one night.

Act I

(Curtain opens. Total darkness on stage.
Pause
A man's voice speaks in the darkness.)

MAN'S VOICE: Where does the beast live, you ask.
Look within your own heart.

(Pause
Loud ticking of the clock is heard in the darkness.
Pause
One light focuses on the grandfather clock on the wall which shows eight o'clock and tolls eight times.
As action starts on stage, ticking of the clock subsides and light on the clock fades out.
Dim lights light the stage.
Night time. Darkness outside the windows.
No one on stage.
Frantic knocking is heard on an unseen door left.
No activity on stage.
Knocking repeats and then becomes continuous.
Mathew runs on the stage through the right archway, runs to the left window, looks out, and runs out through the left archway.
Sounds of heavy bolts being drawn are heard.

Vikram runs on to the stage from the left archway. He is holding an expensive leather overnight case in one hand and dragging Reema by her wrist with the other.

Reema has a designer label handbag slung on one shoulder.

Mathew runs in behind them.

Vikram is agitated.

Reema's lips are set in a mocking smile.

Vikram comes to a dead stop in the centre of the stage. Mathew almost runs into him, stops, staggers and pulls back.)

VIKRAM: *(Turning to Mathew, in a rushing, agitated manner)*

We were on our holiday –

REEMA: *(Interrupting Vikram, to Mathew)*

He means *he* was on holiday.

VIKRAM: *(Looking at her bemused)*

What the...

REEMA: *(Still to Mathew, sarcastically)*

For me every day is a holiday; or so he tells me all the time.

VIKRAM: *(Vikram frowns and turns back to Mathew)*

driving to that new hotel up on the hill –

REEMA: *(To Mathew, interrupting Vikram again, arching her eyebrows and twisting her neck)*

A seven-star hotel. Verrry expensive.

VIKRAM: *(Ignoring her, still to Mathew)*

when this group of people came down the road running for their lives, shouting there was an armed gang coming down the road killing everybody, burning everything in its way. Turn back, turn back, they shouted running across the fields.

REEMA: *(In general, to nobody in particular)*

So we turned back. We are gullible; also cowards.

(Vikram jerks her wrist, glances angrily at her and turns back to Mathew)

VIKRAM: And then, a few miles down the road, another group of people came running up the road shouting there was another armed gang coming up the road. Get off the road, they will kill you, they shouted. Then a young boy pointed towards this lane. There is a Christian resort down there by the riverside, go there, he shouted while running.

REEMA: *(Shrugging her shoulders in resignation)*

So we came here.

(Looking around and wrinkling her nose in disgust, sarcastically, in general to everybody)

And now we are safe.

(Vikram glares at her.
She jerks her wrist free, throws her handbag on the sofa and moves away.
Mathew, who has been looking from one to the other, now holds his hands up.)

MATHEW: *(To Vikram)*

Calm down, calm down, that was just a rumour. These villagers, you can never trust them, you know. They have nothing else to do but gossip. So they just sit around and distort and exaggerate and then spread every rumour they come across. And they are so stupid that then they start believing in those rumours themselves! Relax, relax. The Home Minister himself has assured the people that he has the situation well under control.
(Raises his eyebrows, looks impressed, and nods a couple of times.)
He was on TV just a little while ago, you see, asking people to keep calm and not believe any rumours of this
(Drawing his shoulders back and imitating a pompous voice)

'impending countrywide communal violence'.

(Vikram looks at him sceptically.
Mathew nods again reassuringly at Vikram and
then looks around for Reema but she has turned
her back to him and so turns back to Vikram.)

MATHEW: Relax. You are perfectly safe here. This resort is quite a bit off the main highway as you know, closer to the river. And it *is* known as a Christian resort; and those gangs – even if there are any – would be of Hindus and Muslims wanting to kill each other. So why would they come here? They are not interested in killing us poor Christians. So don't worry, don't worry at all. Just relax.
(Offering his hand)
Mathew, owner of this resort.

VIKRAM: *(Ignoring his hand)*

Are you sure? They positively won't come here?

(Mathew, a little deflated, drops his hand, looks at Vikram's expensive overnight case and adopts an ingratiating manner.)

MATHEW: Of course, of course, Sir, they definitely won't come here. You can depend on it. In any case it is too far in from the highway for them, you see. You just relax here for a few days

until all this talk of riots subsides. This is a very pleasant resort with all sorts of facilities. There is also a nice walk down to the river. And don't worry, Sir. Nobody comes here.
(Sadly shaking his head, to himself)
Nobody ever comes here.

VIKRAM: *(Relieved)*

Oh!
(Sits on the sofa, spreads his arms on its back and crosses his legs in a relaxed manner and looks benignly at Mathew mollified by his servile manner.)

Actually, these rumours of communal riots spreading all over the country have been rife for quite a while but nobody knew anything for sure. Still, given the mood of the workers in my factories, I thought we might as well close down for a couple of days and take a short holiday; get out of the town; and escape the violence too in case it happens. But I couldn't get away from my desk till the last minute and...
(Shrugs his shoulders. Looks around the lounge and clamps his lips in disapproval.)
Well, left it a bit late, I guess.

(Reema, who has been moving languidly around the stage, comes to the window and stands looking out.)

REEMA: There is a village across there!

VIKRAM: *(In panic again, jumping up.)*

16

Village? Village? What village?
(Goes to the window, peers over Reema's shoulder and turns to Mathew.)
What village is that? A Hindu village or a Muslim one?

MATHEW: *(Throwing his left arm out)*

That half is Hindu.
(Throwing his right arm out)
And that half is Muslim. Have a look.

(Switches on a few more lights brightening the room and emphasising the darkness outside the windows.)

VIKRAM: *(In panic)*

No. No. Put off the lights, put off the lights. And pull the curtains close.

REEMA: *(To Mathew)*

You see, if we can't see them, then they can't see us.
(Patting her hair and rubbing her arms)
I want a wash.

(Mathew dims the lights and moves back.)

MATHEW: *(To Vikram)*

It's ok, Sir, it's ok. That village is deserted now. Everybody ran away this evening when

the rumours of the riots and the killings started. Where are they going to run to that is safer than here, you tell me. Stupid cowards. Afraid of their own shadows. One little rumour comes their way and they all run away.
(Pause
In a peeved manner)
All my staff also. All the boys and girls. Everybody ran away at the first rumour.

(Mathew shakes his head in resignation. Vikram is still jittery, keeps glancing out of the window.)

REEMA: *(To Mathew)*

Oh, don't mind him.
(Bending towards Mathew, in a confiding tone, loudly)
It's just that he
(Flicking her head towards Vikram)
is feeling a little lost because he can't call his Hindu fundamentalist brother for help. His cell phone isn't working. That too a verrrry expensive, latest model.
(Straightening up, in a false pompous manner)
Imported.

(Vikram has taken a last look out of the window and then satisfied, drawn the curtain, moved to the sofa, and is sitting down.)

VIKRAM: *(Sullenly, to Reema)*

He would have got us out of here if I could have got to him. He has the resources. And the manpower. He wouldn't have left us stranded in a dump like this in the middle of nowhere.

REEMA: *(To Vikram, sarcastically)*

May be one of those gangs was his gang come to rescue us. And now you have run away from them! And if what Mathew here says is true, then they will never find us in this black hole. What a joke!

(Vikram looks about uncertainly.
Mathew is watching the whole scene with concern.)

REEMA: *(To Mathew)*

Oh don't worry. He
(Flicking her thumb at Vikram)
isn't one of those fanatics. He worries only about money. And power.
(Leaning towards Mathew, continuing in the same loud confiding tone)
Actually, he is an opportunist.

MATHEW: *(Hurriedly, before Vikram can react)*

Let me show you to your room. In fact you can have your pick of the rooms. There is nobody else here except a Mr and Mrs Joseph. And they are in a cottage.
This way, this way.

(He gestures up the stairs. Reema looks up and then goes up the stairs and through the archway on the landing. Mathew turns to Vikram.)

MATHEW: Let me carry your bag, Sir.

VIKRAM: *(Gets up but hesitates)*

Are you sure we are safe here?

MATHEW: *(Nodding vigorously)*

Of Course, of course, Sir. Absolutely safe. That was just a rumour. And even if those villagers are right, no way any of those rioters will ever come looking for a *Christian* resort so much out of their way. They will just concentrate on those Hindu or Muslim ones on the highway. Just relax, Sir, just relax.

(Vikram gives him a long look then nods looking satisfied, climbs one step, stops, then turns and bends slightly towards Mathew.)

VIKRAM: *(In a low voice)*

Actually it's my wife – she doesn't show it but deep down she worries, you see. Unnecessarily, I think; but what can you do? Women! You know.

(Vikram gives Mathew a long look and then turns

and starts up the stairs with Mathew following with his bag.
Behind them Salim comes in through the right archway, leans against its side and stands watching their backs.)

MATHEW: Of course, of course, Sir. Nothing to worry about here. Madam should just relax, just relax. I will give you our best room. It has a wonderful view of the river.

(Vikram and Mathew go up the stairs and through the archway.
Lights brighten on the stage.
Salim goes to the window, draws the curtain back and stands looking out singing softly to himself.
Pause
Jai walks in from the right archway and moves around aimlessly.
Salim glances at him and turns back to the window.
Jai touches a few curios then looks at the handbag lying on the sofa.)

JAI: New guests?

SALIM: Yeah. A couple. Rich, I would say from the way Mathew was fawning all over them.

(Jai picks up the handbag by looping a finger through its strap and studies it critically while twirling it around.)

JAI: Super-rich, I would say. This handbag is

from the top of the line with the logo, the designer's name and the owner's initials too engraved in the leather.

SALIM: *(Turning around to look at Jai and raising an eyebrow)*

Your class enemy?

JAI: *(Smiles wryly)*

From where I stand at the moment, in the pits of pits, everybody seems to be classes above me. Too high up even to be an enemy. Anyway, good for Mathew. Where is he going to accommodate them? In the store room?

(Salim guffaws and turns back to the window. Jai lets the handbag drop back on the sofa, moves to the sideboard, picks up a newspaper, looks at the headlines and then throws it down and goes and sprawls down on the sofa chair.)

JAI: *(With a sigh)*

This damn emergency! Wish it would all be over one way or another. I am going stir-crazy just sitting around cooped up in here like a chicken in a cage.

SALIM: *(Still looking out, curtly)*

You have been here hardly a day, Jai. I have

been here for the better part of a week; since the border-crossing became unsafe.

JAI: You can sing your time away, Salim. I have nothing to do here and plenty to do back in the jungle. I have *got* to get back there soon.

SALIM: How?
(Turns to look at him and leans his back against the window frame.)
The police are out there everywhere Jai; you have no way out of here. Every airport, every railway station, every bus depot is under watch. There are check-posts every few kilometres on the highways. And all the major routes all over the country are patrolled.

JAI: Especially the border. The *whole* length of it. *You* really are stuck here.

SALIM: *(Looking into the distance)*

This state of emergency can't last forever. The border will become porous again. Loopholes will appear in every precaution.
(Looks back at Jai)
Then we both can leave.

JAI: Good of you to offer to share your cottage with me, Salim, when that idiot Mathew kept saying that the resort was full; though it was stupid of me to get caught here like this with no safe route back into the jungle. Comrades kept telling me not to come here at this time but it was important to attend this meeting; *particularly* at this time.

SALIM: *(Shrugs, still curtly)*

Doesn't matter where you went once you left your jungle; nowhere was safe for you. They are expecting countrywide violence.

JAI: All the same, thanks for helping me out. What a surprise it was to find you here of all the places and after all these years. I would have been in a real mess if you hadn't offered me a bed on the sofa in your cottage. There was nowhere else to go at that time of the night.

(Salim just keeps looking at him.)

JAI: *(Putting up his hands)*

I know, I know, we *were* close friends in college. But that was a decade ago. And we haven't met since then or even kept in touch since – well, since I joined up with the Naxalites. And you *knew* that. Not many of our past friends with *that* knowledge would have been so generous.

SALIM: I didn't know for a long time. And when I did come to know, it didn't surprise me.

JAI: Because I come from the same area, from the
                  same people?

SALIM: No. Because by then I knew that the social
                  justice that you were seeking legally was an
                  impossibility, just a pipedream.

                  (Jai looks at him silently.)

SALIM: And now *you* know who I have joined up
                  with during this last decade.

JAI: All the more reason to avoid me.

SALIM: *(Looking coldly at him)*

                  All the more reason to keep you under my
                  eye. Maybe I just wanted to keep you close
                  to me once you recognised me.
                  (Smiles tightlipped)
                  There is a price on my head as you know.

JAI: *(Looking thoughtfully at him)*

                  Salim the Muslim terrorist might want to. But
                  not the Salim I knew, not the Salim I saw
                  just now standing at the window singing to
                  himself. That Salim cared for his friends.

SALIM::   *(Coldly)*

                  That Salim is dead. That Salim died a long
                  time ago.

JAI: Yet you still sing. And you *did* offer to share
                        your cottage with me.

SALIM: *(To himself, looking reflectively into the distance)*

                        This ability to sing is the only thing that has
                        kept me sane in this mad world.
                        (To Jai, coldly again)
                        It was just camaraderie, Jai. Right now we
                        both are in the same boat.

JAI: *(Looking away)*

                        Yeah. Also in a larger sense, both in sinking
                        ships. Fighting for lost causes.

SALIM: *(Turns to him surprised.)*

                        So you have finally accepted that a totally
                        classless society cannot exist? But what about
                        a peasants-and-workers-controlled Indian
                        State? Hasn't an armed revolution to achieve
                        that been your aim all along?

JAI: What are revolutions, Salim? They revolve;
                        and they revolve within a structure but they
                        never change the structure – our pyramidal
                        social structure of hierarchy and pecking
                        order. And in that structure this revolution
                        takes place only in the top half of it. They
                        bring middle classes to the top and top
                        classes to a lower level but the bottom
                        class – the most oppressed layer – is not even

ruffled. Which revolution has ever made any difference to them?

(Leaning forward)

French Revolution; liberty, equality, fraternity. The aristocrats got their heads chopped off but the peasants only became poorer, hungrier and more miserable. Lenin never cared for peasants in spite of his slogan 'Alliance of workers and peasants' and his policies in Russia only led to forced labour and the Bread War. In China, Mao himself had admitted that the benefits of the revolution had not reached the rural areas and his Great Leap Forward proved to be a disaster.

Power does corrupt, Salim. And then we are the same people whether at the top or lower below. What use is a revolution? Does it really make a difference who is at the top?

(Ruminating)

Anyway, communism is being revised all over the world –

(Salim raises an eyebrow)

JAI: *(Putting up a hand)*

Yeah, I know; capitalism is also in crisis. And socialism has meant License Raj for us.
But still, communism is definitely not ever going to rule here in whatever version they may present it.

SALIM: You believe that and yet you carry on. Why?

JAI:

Because a man must do what he believes in. And I have always believed in the cause of the downtrodden – even in our college days – you know that. We have had all-night discussions about it though at that time I had thought of fighting only legally for their rights. When that dream was shattered, Naxalites seemed to be the only ones around who cared for their upliftment.

(Pause)

I carry on because I work with the tribals at a micro level, at that lowermost level, not at the macro level and the tribals trust me. They are caught between the deep sea and the hard rock, Salim. Every day they are losing more and more of their ancestral land – *their* land to which they have no rights. The Forest Rights Act is an eyewash, Salim. In practice, it's more violated than applied.

And I am allowed to carry on by the die-hard Naxalites because though I am not a hardcore member, I am still useful to them.

(Laughs)

And also because they can always use me as a showpiece for the journos.

(Looks up at Salim, then suddenly gets up and goes to stand by the sideboard looking into the distance.

Salim watches him silently.)

(Seriously, hesitantly, still looking away from Salim)

A decade is a long time to watch and understand, Salim. The Naxalites won't get anywhere with the tribals because they don't heed their sensibilities; they don't understand the tribals – their social system, their traditions, their mentality. They are not creating mass resistance; they are just enrolling them in an anarchist army.

I am in a quandary, Salim. There are times when I wonder whether this path that I am on is the right one. I don't know.

(Pause

Salim looks on sympathetically.

Jai turns and looks at him and then laughs wistfully.)

At one time they could have stopped this Naxalite advance in tribal areas in one day if they would have just restricted the mining, concentrated on land conservation, sincerely applied the Forest Rights Act and provided basic amenities at the grass root level; and then, most importantly, just left the tribals alone to make their own choices, find their own pace towards development; not tried to force them in their mould.

(Salim looks sceptical.)

JAI: *(Earnestly)*

They really could have, you know, Salim. But in this country of ours nobody cares for the unseen ones.

SALIM: Yeah? And would those benefits have sufficed to counter the Communist ideology?

JAI:

Do you think the masses believe in Communist ideology? Or even understand what it means to overthrow the Indian State? You think the peasants in Russia or China understood what one party state meant? They fought for land, for their livelihood and for the freedom to live without somebody beating or raping them. And they all also wanted the development, the conveniences, the material goods. In Russia they were told that come revolution and everybody will be eating strawberries. That's what goaded them on.

(Laughs)

Even Khomeini had promised free housing, free gas, electricity and water *and* free public transport to the Iranians to promote his revolution.

(Laughing wildly)

In Zimbabwe, the promise was that after the revolution every man will get 500 head of White man's best cattle.

(Salim watches him silently.

Jai's laughter peters out and he has a forlorn look.)

Never believe a politician's promise, Salim. It is only rhetoric.

SALIM:

(More as a statement than a question)

And you still believe that violence is the only way you have to uplift the tribals.

JAI:

There is violence and there is violence; depends on how you use it. We have to make

ourselves strong enough so that people pay
attention to us. The government's apathy
towards the tribals has been appalling.
They didn't even know the tribals existed
until the Naxalites started recruiting them
and threatening the exploitation of all those
precious minerals under their land – except
as a curiosity; tribal dances for the visiting
dignitaries with politicians dressed in
tribal costumes.
(Shakes his head)
My god!

SALIM: *(Smiles coldly)*

Don't let the comrades hear you invoking god.

JAI: *(Flicking his hand)*

A leftover habit from the college days that
meeting you has brought forth.

SALIM: *(Looking into the distance, to himself)*

Old habits don't ever die, however hard you
might try, do they? Neither do old attachments
and old friendships. And they surface at the
most unexpected times.

JAI: *(Ignoring Salim's reminiscence)*

But seriously, Salim, nobody takes or has
ever taken any notice of the weak, pleading

voices, you know that. And the sound of a
gun is always heard clear and loud.
(Pause)
Haven't you also found that, Salim? You also
embrace violence. What is *your* ultimate aim?
The world under one Islamic God?

(Salim's face closes and he turns away.)

SALIM: *(Looking away from Jai)*

I am not concerned with the world. Just some
justice in my own country.

JAI: And who promised you justice? You are
old enough to know there is no justice,
only life.
(Waits for a response.
Salim smiles grimly but does not respond)
What happened with you, Salim? You were
never a religious fanatic. In fact, you were
totally oblivious of religion – your own or
anybody else's.

SALIM: We all were, Jai, in our college days. We all
followed certain rites and rituals when forced
to by our elders on certain holy days but they
never meant anything to any of us. Our interests
in those days, if you remember, had been
planning our glorious-to-be careers, all those
extra-curricular activities and disco dancing.

JAI: *(Smiling wryly)*

Yeah, I remember.
(Pause)
What happened afterwards, Salim?
(Waits looking at Salim.
Salim still does not respond.)
You could still get out of it, you know, if you just happened to fall into it.

(Salim looks at him over his shoulder.)

SALIM: You can never go back home again, Jai. You also know that.

JAI: *(Leaning against the sideboard)*

You can. You have not been identified. A legendary but elusive Muslim killer *perhaps* called Salim, that's all that's known about you. One grainy, shadowy photograph in a newspaper that nobody could have recognised. I hadn't. And we were close friends at one time.
You can still get out of the trap, Salim.

SALIM: *(Turning towards Jai)*

Do you really believe that? That I am in a trap? That I didn't choose my side?

JAI: Whose side are you on, Salim?

SALIM: Of those who have had the short end of justice up to now. Those who are not fanatics, those who wholeheartedly believe in peaceful co-existence, and yet are made to suffer. I fight only to alleviate their pain.

JAI: Yet you are allied with a side. And it is a highly biased side. Same as the other side. They both are fanatics.

SALIM: *(Frowning, pacing the rear of the stage)*

That is the problem isn't it? You don't necessarily always choose a side, sometimes a side chooses you. You need a support structure and it puts you firmly in one camp or the other whether you believe in their jingbang rhetoric or not.
But I have made it a condition to all the fundamentalists of all the hues that I work alone and I carry out the justice only as I think fit and in my own way.

JAI: And they let you?

SALIM: They let me.
(Stopping before Jai and looking steadily at him)
You know it Jai, you also practise it: sometimes you have to make war to achieve peace.

JAI: So it's not Jihad.

SALIM: *(Smiling grimly at Jai)*

Doesn't Jihad also mean fighting injustice and oppression? In any necessary way?

(Salim moves to the window singing softly.
Jai sits back quietly on a chair, looking at Salim's back, ruminating.
Long pause
Mathew comes down the stairs grinning hugely, holding a registration card and counting some currency notes.)

MATHEW: *(To himself)*

Two new guests. And rich too. Will they spend! And they may even stay a few days.

SALIM: *(Turning to him)*

That too in your most expensive room. You gave them a choice of rooms and yet you couldn't find a corner for this gentleman last night. At any cost.

MATHEW: *(In an annoyed tone.)*

I told you, this whole resort had been booked by a marketing company for a salesmen's convention.
(Looks up dreamily)
All the rooms and all the cottages booked. And the conference facility and the meeting rooms also. Wives and children with nothing

to do but eat and drink all day. What a bonanza it would have been.

(Sobers up)

And this evening I get this telegram.

(Searches in his pockets, pulls out a telegram and reads in an official tone.)

'In view of the explosive situation in the country, our convention is hereby cancelled.'

(Gesturing towards Jai, bitterly)

Now this gentleman can have as many rooms as he wants.

(To Salim with unctuous obsequiousness)

You were so generous Mr Joseph, so kind to help him, to offer to accommodate him in your cottage. And also to marry that poor unfortunate Muslim girl. But then we Christians are like that: good Samaritans, kind, charitable, unselfish –

SALIM: *(Cutting him short and gesturing upstairs)*

Who are they?

MATHEW: *(Looks at the registration card in his hand, pulls his shoulders back and reads from it in an impressed tone)*

Mr Vikram Dixit and Mrs Namrata Dixit.

(Salim looks at Jai raising his eyebrows. Jai shrugs.)

JAI: Honeymooners?

MATHEW: Ha! Do they look like honeymooners? They said they were on their way to a seven star hotel for a holiday but –
(Suddenly breaks off. In an indignant and puffed up manner)
A dump! A dump and a black hole they called my resort! Is this a dump, I ask you.

(Salim smiles amusedly. Mathew glances at him and goes on defensively)

MATHEW: I re-furbished and renovated all of it last year when I bought this resort. I repainted everything. The money I have spent on it! Look at it now!
(Beaming and grandly gesticulating around)
Look, look at the paintings, the carpets, the chandelier –

JAI: *(Smothering his laugh and putting up his hand)*

Yeah, sure we see. So why are they here in this dump – uh, resort?

MATHEW: They had nowhere else to go. Villagers running down the road told them to turn back because a violent gang was coming down the road and when they turned back, other villagers running up the road said another violent gang was coming up the road.
(Disgustedly)
Rumours. These damn villagers have

nothing else to do but spread each and every unconfirmed rumour they come across.

(Brightens)

But that did get this couple scared and they turned off the road. And now, thank the Lord, they are here.

(Stops in consternation)

Jesus! They will want food and all my boys and girls ran away at the first rumour –

(Rushes off through the rear doorway. Salim has been standing transfixed.)

SALIM: So it has started.

JAI: No. It's just a rumour as Mathew said.

SALIM: The whole country has been simmering for some time now. Rumours have been quite widespread. Something has to boil over.

JAI: No. The government has had enough time to control it.

(Doubtfully)

Unless...

SALIM: Unless it has a vested interest in letting it happen.

JAI: I still don't believe it. Masses aren't that stupid. They can't be manipulated that easily.

SALIM: *(Turning on him, aggressively)*

Masses aren't? What is mass hysteria, Jai? Haven't you ever seen the masses incited into a hysteria by your comrades, by a politician, by any fanatic? What happens to them then, Jai? Don't they all generate a righteousness for a common cause, a common fear, or just a frenzy towards anything at all? Doesn't being part of a mob give normal men a freedom from all moral or social restraints? A freedom that leads them into an irrational behaviour, a mindless violence? Doesn't it lead them to do things in a crowd that they would never do on their own?

JAI: *(Obstinately)*

I still have enough trust in the common sense of the masses. They would rise against a definitely unjust act or for a definite purpose. Not mindlessly as has been rumoured. Do you mean to say people have no will of their own?

SALIM: *(With an ironic smile)*

You have always been and still are a die-hard idealist, Jai.

JAI: So?

(Pause)

SALIM: *(Shrugs)*

Perhaps you are right. Perhaps it is nothing but a rumour, another one of those making the rounds. There have been quite a number of them around recently. Why not this one also?

(Salim turns back to the window singing softly. Jai stares at his back for a while and then runs to the TV.)

SALIM: *(Glancing over his shoulder)*

No good. It went off the air right after the Home Minister assured the people that he had the situation well under control. And so has the radio. And the phones are dead too. I checked.

(Jai checks in mid-stride and stops in his place for a moment.)

JAI: My mobile –

(Runs out through the right archway.
Salim shakes his head and turns back to the window singing to himself.
Long pause
Reema comes down the stairs.
Salim looks up.)

SALIM: *(Startled)*

Reema!

(Reema stops immobile on the last step for a long moment and reaches for the handrail as if needing support and then slowly comes down the step and faces him.)

REEMA: Salim? Salim?

(They stand staring incredulously at each other. Reema is leaning against the railing as if unable to support herself.
Salim's face has changed. Coldness has gone out of it and he suddenly looks vulnerable.)

REEMA: I heard you singing as I came down the stairs; but then I hear you singing all the time and everywhere. When I see a field of flowers; when I see children cavorting merrily; when I see clouds passing; everywhere I hear your voice singing, floating over them all.

SALIM: *(Overcome with emotion)*

Those were songs of love, of hope, and of joy of life that I used to sing. I used to sing of change to a beautiful reality. I used to open my arms wide and sing to the whole wide world. And you used to dance to my songs, dance like a free bird soaring high in the sky, like a sprite in a forest. I could sing of freedom because you gave a meaning to my songs.
Now I sing only to myself, Reema. And I sing of pain, and of incredible ache, and of despair. I sing because if I don't sing it away,

my heart won't be able to contain all that agony and would explode into smithereens.

REEMA: I danced like that because your songs set me free. Listening to your singing I felt I could do anything I wanted, go anywhere I wanted. I had the power to be myself. Your singing gave me wings to soar high. I used to fly to your songs. I don't fly anymore, Salim. I am rooted in the mire now; and the more I try to pull myself out of it, the deeper it pulls me inside it.

(Resting the back of her head against the railing)
How I have been dreaming of you, longing for you, yearning, yearning for you, how unbearable has the ache in my heart been at times, Salim. I kept on remembering, remembering, until – until I gave up on remembering. I couldn't endure it any more. At times I thought I would go out of my mind. Oh, Salim.

SALIM: I too saw you everywhere, dancing, dancing in the fields, dancing in a crowd, dancing on the clouds. I too kept remembering the past, Reema, until the memories became unbearable. Then I learned to suppress them far down in a place in my mind from where no emotion could ever again surface. And then, out of the blue, you walk down those stairs and break that dam in one stroke.

(Pause
A man's voice is heard reciting in the background.

Salim and Reema stay absolutely still maintaining their positions.)

MAN'S VOICE: *(Reciting)*

Do you remember Priyanka,
   those trysts in the nights,
the moon roving in the skies,
and the stars shining in our eyes.

(Pause)

REEMA: I have been searching for you for so long, Salim. I searched everywhere, asked everybody, followed all the leads. I searched and searched for you until there was nowhere left to search.

SALIM: *(Soberly)*

I know.

REEMA: *(Startled, straightens up)*

You know? You know, Salim? Yet you never contacted me. You knew I had been searching for you, yet you never came to me. Were you running away from me all this time? Would you have left here also had you known I was here?

(Salim involuntarily moves towards her and then checks himself.)

SALIM: *(Trying to control himself)*

I think so Reema; if I could have. But I didn't know. Mathew said Vikram and *Namrata* Dixit.

REEMA: *(Turning away)*

They changed my name during the marriage. I am Namrata now.

SALIM: *(Laughing incredulously)*

From Reema to Namrata! From a sword wielding goddess to Namrata; Namrata the meek one!

(Shakes his head.)

REEMA: *(With a flare of temper)*

And what about you? Mathew said only Josephs are here. Are you Joseph?

SALIM: *(Sobers up)*

Temporarily.

(Reema stares at him stupefied)

REEMA: What?

(Jai comes in through the right archway fiddling with his mobile.)

JAI: The mobiles are also jammed. There is no way

left to communicate with the outside world. I still believe that it only means that the government is just trying to stop these wild rumours from spreading. It has been done before in emergencies. Relax, Salim. It was only a –

(Looks up and stops in his tracks on seeing Reema.)

Reema!

REEMA: *(Startled)*

Jai! Well, well, well! What's this, a college alumni get-together?

(Salim laughs – a free and almost happy laugh. Jai looks at him startled and then glances at Reema.)

SALIM: *(Still laughing)*

And none here under his or her rightful name.

(To Jai, flicking his chin at Reema)

She is Namrata now.

REEMA: *(Looking wide eyed at Jai)*

You too Jai? You too have changed your name?

JAI: *(Flicking his hand, deprecatingly)*

A minor change, Reema, just an addition of an

	A. I am not Jaikisan – victory to Lord Krishna – anymore; but Jaikisaan – victory to the farmer.
SALIM:	A minor change with major repercussions.
REEMA:	*(Looking at Salim in incomprehension)*
	What?
	(Then realises, and shocked, retreats a little, leans her back on the staircase railing.)
	Jaikisaan! Jaikisaan the Naxalite! The one who is always in the news; always caught on the camera with his back to it and his head covered with a towel.
	(Sadly)
	Oh Jai, what happened to you? How did you get into it? You were going to be a lawyer, a social justice lawyer. And Salim was going to be a singer singing songs of social significance, of freedom.
JAI:	And you were going to be an investigative journalist, investigating all the social evils.
REEMA:	What happened to us all?
JAI:	*(In a light manner)*
	Well at least you are always in the news if not the creator of it. In the Society News pages.
REEMA:	And Salim was the one I had expected to see in the news all the time. Being mobbed

by his fans. But he never has been. He just disappeared.

SALIM: *(With a rueful smile)*

That Salim did.

(Reema looks at him.)

REEMA: *(Looking into the distance, sadly repeating)*

What happened to us all? We were such idealists in college. How did we all end up like this? What dreams we had at one time – those all-night discussions and arguments about exploitative politics, those hours-long sessions writing songs, listening to Salim set them to music, those days in the library and surfing on the net to get the info, all those big plans, and look where we all have ended up.
(Turns to Jai)
What happened to you Jai?

JAI: What happened to me? What happened? What do I tell you, Reema?

(Blackout for a moment.
Then only the footlights on the balcony come on to shine upwards on Jai standing on the balcony.
In the shadowy light on the rest of the stage, Salim and Reema stay stock-still maintaining their positions.)

JAI: After my graduation in law I went back to my people to tell them to eschew violence, to resort to law and reason. This is a new age, I told them, this is an age of equality, of democracy, of power to people. I will be your spokesperson, I said, in me you have the resource you have lacked until now; I will open those closed doors of justice to you.

But when the exploiters came, they came with sticks and guns and torches, attended by the executors of law. I spoke of equality and liberty and the answer came out of the mouth of a gun.

(Pause
A man's voice is heard reciting in the background.
Jai stands absolutely still frowning angrily.)

MAN'S VOICE: *(Reciting)*

The answer came out of the mouth of a gun.

A red splash on the pavement,
a lingering sigh of the last breath
and to the unyielding sky a hand raised.
That's all that of him remained.

For long after they took him away,
the imprint of his hand still stayed
etched in the air
trembling in the wind
stretching towards the passersby as if to say,

Take this message, brothers,
take it just a little further on.

(Pause)

JAI: And they laughed at me. I tried to reason with them and they burned my house. I talked of law and they jailed me.

In the jail it was more kicks, punches and questions – questions, questions and questions. Who else is part of your gang, where are your arms depots? Who are your friends, parents, wife? Why don't you have any children? Any lovers – male or female? What is it that you like, don't like, hate? Who and where and what all the time but never, never the why of it; that, they did not want to hear.

Eventually they kicked me out of the jail. Go home to your wife, they said. But my home was burnt and my wife was dead.

(Jai smiles a little sadly, a little ironically at the memory.)

Then I knew that all that they would ever hear, all that they would ever respond to, was the return sound of the gun. Only a brutal force would wrest out of them what was rightfully ours: our land, our rights, and our dignity.

My people were wise; they had always known it.

(Blackout for a moment.

Then lights come on as before and all three are in the same positions as before.)

JAI: *(To Reema)*

Reality killed my dreams. What happened to you?

REEMA: Reality was too much for me. So I killed myself.

(Mathew rushes in from the rear-left door)

MATHEW: Mr Joseph, Mr Joseph, please make your wife understand. We have guests. They will want food.

(Shanaz comes in behind him and stands with one hand raised along the doorframe, other on her waist, her hip sticking out – an overtly sexy posture.)

SHANAZ: Cook, he says. Why should I cook? Am I a cook? Cook for the guests, he says. I am also a guest here.

(Reema is staring at her shocked.
Salim is watching Reema.
Jai looks uncomfortably from Reema to Salim.)

JAI: Living the way I do, one learns all sorts of skills.

(To Mathew)

Let's see what we can do.

(Jai hustles Shanaz and Mathew out through the door at the rear.)

REEMA: *(Dazed, still staring at the spot where Shanaz had been standing.)*

She is a prostitute!

SALIM: *(Still watching her)*

Perhaps. But not necessarily. Shanaz was a bar dancer before.

REEMA: *(Turns to Salim)*

Same difference.

SALIM: For some of them, yes, but not for all.

(Reema keeps looking at him.)

SALIM: Shanaz was only a dancer, Reema, a dancer in a bar, until the bar was closed by the police. Then she too had to find a patron for survival.

(Reema still keeps looking at him, waiting.)

SALIM: She is pregnant, Reema. Hazard of profession. But her patron has refused to let her have an abortion. He wants that baby. He says he will take his son away after his birth and then he will leave her free and rich. But she neither wants to go through nine months of it nor can she afford to be saddled with a child in case he reneges on his word. More than anything else, she didn't want to bear his baby. But she still needed his patronage. She was in a dilemma, Reema.

REEMA: *(Still in a daze)*

Didn't want, needed, was – all in the past. So you have married her and solved her dilemma! You are married to a prostitute!

SALIM: *(Gravely)*

I have made a business arrangement with her. I have hired her to pose as Mrs Joseph for a few days. She will be well off at the end of it. She will be able to afford not only the abortion but much more also. She can be independent again.

REEMA: Why? Why? Why do you need a sham wife?

SALIM: A couple is less suspicious, more acceptable than a single man in a resort.

REEMA: *(Startled)*

Are you in hiding, Salim? Who from? What's going on? What's this 'Joseph' about? Why do you need to be Joseph?

(Salim keeps looking at her but doesn't reply. Reema stares back at him for a long moment and then slowly backs to a chair and sits down covering her face with her hands.)

REEMA: *(In anguish, shaking her head)*

No, No, No! I won't believe it. I won't, I won't. I won't. It's not true. You are *not* that dreaded Muslim terrorist Salim!

SALIM: *(Still gravely)*

You knew, Reema, you always knew.

REEMA: *(Looks up, a devastated look. Then straightens her shoulders)*

Yes, I knew.

SALIM: No one else recognised me in that murky photograph in the newspaper but I knew you would.

REEMA: *(Turning away)*

Yes, I knew. But I refused to acknowledge it. *(Pause)*
I hoped against all hope that I was wrong. I wouldn't admit it even to myself, even in my deepest subconscious. I thought if I refused to accept it, it will turn out to be untrue.

(Jumping up and accosting Salim, grabbing him by his arms and shaking him violently)
Why, Salim, why? And don't give me that cliché about my marriage having led you into it.

(Salim gently loosens her hands and stares at her still holding her hands, remembering.
Blackout for a moment.
Then only the footlights on the balcony come on to shine upwards on Salim standing on the balcony.
In the shadowy light on the rest of the stage Reema stays stock-still.)

SALIM: When I heard Reema was married, I ran far away, as far as I could, far into the mountains. There, as I sat high up in the clouds singing of the unbearable pain in my heart, locals directed me to an old dervish – two mad men together, they said. I found him singing and dancing on a grassy ridge, an old man with a flowing white beard and a mane of long white hair. I knocked on your heart's door, he said, but you were too deep in your grief to hear your soul answer me. He was a Sufi.

For six months I sat at his feet learning from him and for the first time I understood the love, the mysticism, the compassion in Islam. I came down the mountain singing of love and beauty and walked smack bang into the reality of life, the violence of life.

That violence probed my marrow and wrenched my soul out and twisted and

wrung it like a wet rag leaching out all the feelings, leaving an empty shell behind.
And then something dies in you: love and beauty.

(Blackout for a moment.
Then lights come on as before and both Reema and Salim are in same positions as before.)

SALIM: Well, your father did oppose our marriage only because I am a Muslim.

REEMA: *(Turning away)*

Just the thought of it gave him a heart attack. I was told we were going to that old Shankara Math on Mount Abu to pray for his recovery.

SALIM: When I heard you were gone, I ran to your house. There was a blind beggar sitting outside your gate playing his *ektari* and singing. He told me you were gone though not where or when or what for; but he was singing a wedding song.

REEMA: They all knew but me. Vikram's family was already there, all prepared, waiting for us. There, in that Math on the mountain top in Abu, they told me I would be killing Daddy if I didn't go through the marriage ceremony. They told me that there was a great stress on his mind that wasn't allowing his heart to recoup, that I had to make a quick decision, that there wasn't much time left for Daddy. Look at your mother, look into her red, swollen eyes, they said, and then tell us if you are ready to carry the guilt of wiping the kumkum off her forehead on your shoulders for the rest of your life.

Then Daddy packed us off to his tea estate in Assam.

SALIM: *(Dryly)*

He is very healthy still.

REEMA: Yes.
                (Pause
                In pain)
                Then why, Salim?

SALIM: I was caught in the last communal riots.

REEMA: Oh my god, Salim. Were you – Oh god! Are you ok? That must have been – Oh hell!

                (Reema sits down holding her head in her hands.
                Pause
                After a while Reema gets up, goes to Salim and holds his arms tenderly.)

                Salim, I can feel what you must have gone through. I do understand what it would do to you, Salim, believe me, I do. I can see what must have happened –

SALIM: *(Interrupting her, harshly)*

Can you? Can you visualise it all? That mad frenzy, those murderous shouts, those jubilant cries of the killers, those explosions that shake your bones, those groans of the dying, that rasp of the last breath so close to your ear –

REEMA: *(Shaking him)*

Saliiim!

(Salim looks at her as if in a daze, then shakes his head.)

SALIM: No, you are wrong. I was not in a daze then. Your senses are extra sharp at such times but the meaning of it doesn't sink in. That time you are too busy just staying alive. It's only later, much later, when your body starts healing, that you realise what you had been reduced to and what all had been questioned: your status as a human being for one. And then, Reema, you become something else and you can never go back to what you were.

REEMA: *(Shaking her head vehemently)*

No. No. No! Nobody can inflict that on you, Salim. No one can dehumanise you. Not unless you allow them to do it.

SALIM: *(Turning away from Reema, coldly)*

That's what they say. It is one thing to intellectually discuss it, quite another to actually suffer it.

(Remembering)

They kept asking us to beg; that's what they wanted from us. Beg, you dirty *Musalman*, beg for your life now, that's what they kept on shouting. And the more we wouldn't beg, not always out of bravery but because most were too far gone or too much in pain even to understand what was being asked of them, the more they would torture us. Sometimes you can die with dignity; sometimes even that is denied to you.

They had given me an identity, a different one from the one I had till then, and it hit hard, harder than one could imagine. That just being a Muslim was enough to invite one's slaughter like a pig.

(Reema stares at him for a moment, then goes and stands against the window bowing her head and resting it on the window jamb.

Pause

After a while Reema lifts her head, squares her shoulders and looks at Salim's back.)

REEMA: That's not a good enough reason either, Salim. You were never one to give in to rantings of some fanatics. You were never naive. You have known about cruelty, about injustice. What happened in those riots was absolutely, deplorably terrible but there were many sane people – Hindus and Muslims – who condemned that massacre, those rapes, those burnings. They appealed to their own to bring calm and sense into that chaos. You could have joined up with them.

SALIM: *(Still with his back to Reema)*

They weren't there. They didn't hear the screams. They didn't scream themselves.

(Blackout for a moment.
Then only the footlights on the balcony come on to shine upwards on Salim standing on the balcony.
In the shadowy light on the rest of the stage Reema stays stock-still maintaining her position.)

SALIM: They came at us with knives and swords. They had not covered their faces. Something happens to you when you look into the killers' faces, into their eyes.
Something happens to you then. The terror engulfs you. Not the terror of death or of torture but the terror of recognising those faces, of understanding what is in those eyes. Suddenly you are too scared to turn around to face them because you know that you will find the same faces that you have been laughing with just yesterday are today laughing at you. The strangers you exchanged smiles with at a party, the people you danced with last night

in a disco, the fans you sang for, the same, the same people are now enjoying tearing you to bits. It's the terror of facing that inhumanity in their eyes that stops you from facing them. But you do.

And when you do face them, something unexpected happens to you. You understand the complicity between the killers and the victims in this act of killing. The complicity that kills all the humanity not only in the killers but also in the victims.

I had invited them that day as surely as fate by singing my heart to them, by baring my soul to them. I had said, come. And now seeing their souls looking at me from their eyes I understood what they were saying. It was, come.

And you know they don't mean you to become one of them, but to exchange the roles.

You become the killer, they the prey.

(Blackout for a moment.
Then lights come on as before and both Salim and Reema are in same positions as before.)

SALIM: Physical wounds heal Reema. What dies within you stays dead.

(Reema goes to him and turns him to face her. Tenderly.)

REEMA: Nobody can understand the pain and suffering of the victim except the victim himself. It's easy for others to advise, to pontificate, but still, there was counselling, Salim. A lot of NGOs went around organising camps, helping –

SALIM: *(Interrupting her)*

I know what they said: 'Get the anger out of you. Don't let it fester. Talk it out, act it out. Forgive and forget.' Do you really believe it helps to cleanse you, to make you remember with equanimity what you have seen and heard and gone through? Does it bring back your belief in humanity, your trust in the basic goodness in people?

REEMA: *(Dropping her hands, dejectedly)*

You were always such a moral person, Salim. You never harmed anybody; you never took advantage of anybody. You had a sense of justice.

SALIM: What is morality, Reema? There is none in the natural order of the world. A snake bites when it feels threatened. A tiger kills when he is hungry. And a crocodile reduces to smithereens any living thing that comes within its reach even when it is not hungry. Morality doesn't enter into it.

REEMA: But they are not sadistic killers; it is a trait peculiar only to the humans.
(Sadly)
And now you have become a killer too.

SALIM: Assassin.

REEMA: *(Looks at him startled.)*

                   What?

SALIM: I choose who I kill. Some people deserve to die.

REEMA: Don't we all?

SALIM: Some people deserve to die sooner than others so that others may live in peace.
(Reema stares at him)
Masses tilt, Reema, and they tilt with fervour towards any charismatic leader preaching violence or peace. And when the preacher promotes violence, then it's the innocents who get sacrificed.
So to have some modicum of peaceful co-habitation, one has to remove those who preach hatred.
(Musing)
It has been said before that if someone had killed Hitler in the thirties, six million Jews would have lived.
(Sobering)
You cut off the head, the body withers.

REEMA: No! You talk as if there is only one beast. But that's not true. A whole populace, all those who follow him, believe in the same things as he. Someone always rises to wear the mantle and lead the same people again.

(Salim stares at Reema.)

SALIM: *(Looking away, to himself)*

Those have been my concerns too. She is expressing my concerns. But then we could always look into each other's hearts, hear the unspoken.
(To Reema)
Perhaps, Reema. But in this chaos of today, sometimes the only cause one has left is to stick to a cause.

(Reema suddenly looks at him with understanding.)

REEMA: And how do you fight terrorism? By becoming a terrorist yourself?

SALIM: You know of any other way?

REEMA: *(Hopelessly, shaking her head)*
There must be. There must be.
(With awe and horror)
You have become a believer!
(Sadly)
I searched for you, I searched for you for so long. I searched everywhere for you. But I was searching for the wrong person.

(Blackout for a moment.

Then only the footlights on the balcony come on to shine upwards on Reema standing on the balcony.

In the shadowy light on the rest of the stage Salim stays stock-still maintaining his position.)

REEMA: What's the matter with me? I know Salim has become a killer and I still love him. I love him dearly, with all my heart, and now that I have found him again, I can't let him go. Can I accept him as he is? I can't, I can't. But I can't live without him either. Oh Salim, Salim.

I have always known Salim has become a killer. I knew it when nowhere could I find a soulful singer called Salim. I knew it when I went to ask his family about him and his family turned their backs on me. I knew it when I saw that grainy, murky photo in the newspaper though I wouldn't acknowledge it even to myself; I refused to believe it. But still, without realising it, it changed me, changed my whole life. Nothing made sense anymore. Not Salim, not me, not life. There was no purpose to anything anymore.

I have lived with the burden of my guilt for so long now. Guilt for believing in Daddy's feigned heart attack, guilt for allowing others to push me into marrying a gold-digger and the guilt – though unacknowledged, but still there – for having led Salim into becoming a killer.

And guilt for what I had let myself become. I, an independent girl who always knew her mind and acted on her own beliefs, who wanted to do something socially relevant with her life, had been reduced to a nincompoop in one stroke.

And as a panacea what I wanted was revenge. Revenge on those whom I blamed for *my* actions. Revenge on Daddy who made me betray Salim, revenge on Vikram who married me only for Daddy's money. Daddy wanted me to be a subdued, submissive housewife concerned only with the house and children so I became what I had always detested: a socialite. I had affairs with everybody on the circuit. Vikram desperately wanted an heir so I ensured I wouldn't be able to bear one. I lost myself in trying to lose my burden of guilt.

But Salim had acted on his own convictions and Daddy had deferred to his own prejudice and Vikram was promoting his own interests. And I? I was merely reacting to what they had done to me.

What I have really done is that I have taken a revenge on myself.

(Blackout for a moment.
Then lights come on as before and Salim and Reema are in the same positions as before.)

REEMA: I cried a river over you, Salim. I cried until there were no more tears to flow; not because my eyes had gone dry but because it was my heart that had dried up.

(Looks straight into Salim's eyes.)

I won't be seeing you again, Salim.

SALIM: *(Soberly)*

No.

REEMA: I will leave you with this promise though. Whatever my life will be in future, it will be that because I want it that way, not as a reaction to someone else's actions – not even yours.

(Salim nods.)

REEMA: And what are you leaving me with, Salim? What do I look forward to? Seeing another photograph of yours in the newspapers lying in the gutter like a dog shot in the back?

(Vikram comes out on the upper landing, stops and stands watching them.)

SALIM: Reema!

REEMA: Oh, Salim, Salim.

(Reema runs over to Salim and wraps her arms around his neck. Salim folds her in his arms and holds her tight.)

VIKRAM: *(Leaning on the railing of the landing)*

Reema! I have heard that name only once before and that was before the marriage. My grandmother said, the girl's name is Reema but we will change it to Namrata.

(Reema and Salim separate.)

VIKRAM: *(Coming down the stairs)*

Reema! Salim!

SALIM: We were together in college.

VIKRAM: *(Sitting down on the sofa)*

Of course. That explains it. Salim! A Muslim! I should have known. A rich and prominent family; the girl so beautiful; a hurried marriage. And me? A struggling middle class accountant. *That* should have opened my eyes.

REEMA: *(Turning to him, with contempt)*

Your eyes were firmly fixed on my father's factories.

VIKRAM: *(Holding himself in control)*

No. I just thought that my merit had finally been appreciated. That a top man had seen the promise in me, had noticed the top qualities in me, had at last recognised my abilities.

REEMA: *(Nastily)*

What abilities? Of wresting the control of the factories away from my father and reducing him to a mere figurehead? Of taking over and pushing him out of his own businesses? Of diverting the funds to your free-loader brother and his group?

VIKRAM: *(Throwing his hands up.)*

Thank god my brother never knew that my wife had an affair with a Muslim.

REEMA: *(Flicking her hand, explaining to no one in particular.)*

His brother is a Hindu fanatic. Belongs to one of those rabid groups.

VIKRAM: *(Suddenly losing his cool, jumping up and glaring at Reema, pointing a finger in her face)*

Don't call him a fanatic. He believes in what he does. And it's not a rabid group. If it hadn't been for him and his group keeping the Muslims in check, we would not have been able to sleep soundly in our beds.

REEMA: *(Unfazed, still to no one in particular)*

He means we Hindus.

VIKRAM: *(Thrusting his face into hers, viciously)*

               Don't tell me what I mean.

REEMA: So where is this saviour brother of yours now
               when we need him?

               *(Salim has moved to the window and is
               looking out. Vikram and Reema are glaring at
               each other.*
               *Shanaz comes in from the rear door, sees Vikram,
               stops dead for a moment surprised, moves back
               a step as if frightened and turns around as if
               wanting to run away. Then pulls herself together,
               takes a deep breath, goes up to him, bends from
               the waist and touches her hand to her forehead in
               Muslim greeting.)*

SHANAZ: Salaam Sahib.

VIKRAM: *(Startled, backing away from Reema.)*

               Chanda!

               *(Reema looks on fascinated. Salim turns from
               the window.)*

SHANAZ: *(Smiling ironically)*

               Shanaz, Sahib, Shanaz. Not Chanda any
               more, Sahib.

VIKRAM: *(Looking down at her and talking superciliously)*

Rubbish! You are not a Muslim. Don't make stupid jokes.

SHANAZ: *Han,* Sahib. I *am* a Muslim.

(Vikram stares at her frowning.
Shanaz pushes up the sleeve of her kameez and shows him a small silver cylindrical amulet tied to her forearm by a thin black cord)

SHANAZ: See this, Sahib? This is a Muslim *taveez*: an Islamic charm for protection against evil intents. Against *all* bad intents, Sahib.
(Looking straight at him)
I am not afraid of you anymore, Sahib.

VIKRAM: *(Staring at the amulet in horror and failing to hear her.)*

So it is true! You *have* become a Muslim!

SHANAZ: *Nahin,* Sahib, I have always been a Muslim. Was born one, Sahib.

VIKRAM: No. No. That can't be true.
(Shaking his head unbelievingly)
No, that's not possible. I know all about you and your family. I know how your uncle grabbed your father's house on his death and threw you out of the house. I know how you were forced to take up that job of a dancer in a bar because you were unskilled to do anything else. I know all about the hard times

you have gone through while dancing in that bar and also after they closed it. You can't fool me. You are Chanda. You are a Hindu girl from a respectable family who –
(Vikram, who had forgotten Reema, now gives a start and glances at her surreptitiously, then continues lamely)
who just needed some help; and I helped you.
(Straightens up.
Sternly)
So stop teasing me. You are going beyond the limits of decency now.

(Shanaz looks nervous for a moment, then looks Vikram squarely in the eye.)

SHANAZ: That's a story I wove for you because that's what *you* wanted to believe, Sahib. That I am a good Hindu girl from a good Hindu family trying to eke out a living by dancing in a bar because of the way my respectable Hindu relatives treated me. Because all Muslims are supposed to be dirty, uncouth and savage.

VIKRAM: What nonsense!
(Indignantly)
Are you saying I said that? I never thought that, so how could I have ever said anything like that? Of course I am as angry as anybody else about all these terrorist attacks by the Islamic fundamentalists and I have always been distrustful of their intentions: pan-Islamism

and all that, and worried about their declaring not only America but also India as their greatest enemy, but never what you said.

SHANAZ: *(Sadly)*

You painted us all with the same brush, Sahib. And you made it clear even if not in the same words I said. You hurt us all, Sahib. And I swallowed it all and kept quiet because I needed you then.

VIKRAM: *(Certain of himself, a little tenderly in spite of himself)*

No. I would never have wanted to hurt you.

SHANAZ: *(Turning away)*

One who hurts never remembers. One who is hurt never forgets.

(Pause
Viciously, turning back to him.)

I hated doing it, Sahib, I can tell you that now, I hated having to hide my birth, my beliefs and my religion from you and from the world, but I needed your patronage after the bar closed. And it was still worth it to see how easily I could fool you, to see that look of bliss come over your face when I told you my sob story. And you fell for it because that's what *you* wanted to hear, wasn't it, Sahib?

(Vikram takes a step back in shock, has again forgotten Reema's presence. Shanaz looks at him with a smile of triumph.)

VIKRAM: *(Shaking his head in disbelief)*

I can't believe you are the same girl. I have never before seen you like this. I have never heard you talk like this. You have always been so well behaved, so docile. So soft spoken and so gentle. You were always so humble, so modest that you hardly ever looked up and never raised your voice. The fact that you were always so diffident, so amenable and so caring was what had attracted me to you in the first place.

SHANAZ: What do you expect from a powerless, needy person, Sahib, if not servitude?
But I am not that needy Shanaz anymore, Sahib, I am not dependent on your money now. So I don't have to pretend, I don't have to kowtow to you anymore, Sahib.
I gave you your money's worth, Sahib. I gave you what you expected. What *I* didn't expect was that you would therefore decide that I was good enough to bear your child.

(Vikram gasps, stares at her for a long moment,

then staggers to the sofa, sits down heavily and covers his face with his hands)

VIKRAM: *(Moaning)*

My son's mother – a Muslim!

(Reema starts laughing crazily)

REEMA: And what is your Hindu fundamentalist brother going to say to *that?*

CURTAIN

ACT II

(Same night, a little later.
Only one light is on and it is focused on the clock on the wall ticking loudly.
The clock shows nine pm and tolls nine times.
A low singing voice is heard in the background.
On the last toll of the clock, the light on the clock goes off and other lights come on.
Ticking of the clock subsides and the singing becomes louder.
Shanaz is singing and dancing a sexy bar-dance swirling her dupatta around, unaware of others, lost in her own dance.
Vikram is sitting on the sofa holding his head in his hands.
Salim standing at the window, Reema seated on the sofa, Jai and Mathew standing by the wall, are watching Shanaz's dance with interest.)

SHANAZ: *(Singing and dancing)*

I have kohl in my eyes
my lips are red
I have bells tinkling around my ankles
and passion rippling through my body.

Come my beloved
while the night is young
for it won't last forever
and it will be dawn too soon.

(Rajesh saunters in from the left archway carrying a plastic briefcase and a small cardboard suitcase, sees Shanaz pirouette and stops in the archway watching her in astonishment. His mouth drops open, his eyes pop and his suitcase drops with a thud disgorging cheap synthetic shirts and trousers.

Shanaz comes out of her trance and stops dancing.

Vikram raises his head.

Everybody turns to look at Rajesh.

Rajesh, startled, looks around, reddens, closes his mouth and squats down to push his clothes back into the suitcase and then swallows and straightens up dusting his clothes and arranges his face suitably.

All eyes curiously follow his every move in silence.)

RAJESH: *(Advancing into the room with a silly grin, false confidence and heartiness)*

Good evening everybody. I am afraid I am here a little late at night but the traffic was quite bad.

(All look back blankly.
Mathew moves forward to face him.)

RAJESH: Oh hello. You are the manager here? I am Rajesh, here for that salesmen's convention. Rest of our people are expected tomorrow morning, aren't they? I hope it is ok for me to come here a night earlier.

(Vikram leans back and looks speculatively at him.
Rajesh walks past Mathew without giving him a chance to speak, looks around and settles on Reema.)

RAJESH: But now that I am already here, let me show you, madam, what our company is offering.

(Sits on a hard chair next to Reema, opens his briefcase and pulls out a catalogue.)

RAJESH: A fabulous range of household articles. See these discounts? And you can also win a frying pan with –

(Reema turns her face away haughtily.
Rajesh, his face fallen, looks around again and sees Shanaz watching him with her arms akimbo and hesitantly approaches her.)

RAJESH: We also have a good range of cosmetics. Perhaps you would be interested –

(Mathew pushes himself in front of Rajesh.)

MATHEW: Your company has cancelled the convention.

RAJESH: *(Looks everybody over in confusion.)*

             Cancelled? Cancelled? But why?

SALIM: *(Laughing)*

Where have you been, kid? Don't you know that the whole country is on the brink of erupting into communal riots?

REEMA: *(Sarcastically)*

Didn't you meet those two gangs of rioters on the road? One coming up the road and the other coming down the road?

RAJESH: *(All his bravado gone.)*

I – I – I came the back way.

SALIM: Through the deserted village?

RAJESH: Well, I – I – I mean...

(Vikram suddenly straightens up)

VIKRAM: How did you get in?

RAJESH: *(Startled)*

What?

VIKRAM: The front door, was it open?

RAJESH: Of course it was open. I mean shouldn't the front door of a resort be open? But there was no one at the reception desk.

VIKRAM: *(Gesturing to Mathew, authoritatively)*

Go close that door. Bolt it. How could you leave the front door open? Hurry up.

MATHEW: It's ok, it's ok. It's only a rumour anyway. The Home Minister himself has said that –

VIKRAM: *(Interrupting him, urgently)*

Didn't you hear me? Go bolt that door. Go!

*(Mathew rushes out through the left archway.
Sounds of bolts being pulled up are heard.
Mathew comes back and stands against the wall.
Vikram relaxes back on the sofa.
Rajesh has watched Mathew go and come back a
little worriedly.)*

RAJESH: You – you don't mean to say that this is really dangerous, this situation?

(Looks suspiciously from one to another.)

I mean you are not just taking me for a ride, are you?

SALIM: *(Seriously)*

No kid, we are not taking you for a ride. There is a rumour making rounds that communal riots are spreading all over the country. Surely you must have heard it. You can't have lived in a vacuum all these days.

RAJESH: But is it true? I mean... Or is it just a rumour? I mean the last time I was at our headquarters I asked them about all this talk I had been hearing about the riots and told them about how my mother had been crying and telling me not to go out of the city anywhere, and they just shrugged and said, 'You just tell us whether you want to keep working here or not. If you want to keep your job with us then you have to make the rounds assigned to you.'
I mean they wouldn't send me out into dangerous areas if it were true, would they?
(Looks around at all the faces.)
They wouldn't, would they?

MATHEW: The Home Minister himself has said that we are not to believe any rumours of this
(Again drawing his shoulders back and imitating a pompous voice)
'impending countrywide communal violence'.

(Looks around at everybody importantly.
Rajesh looks at him unsurely.
Nobody else pays any attention to him.)

SALIM: *(Shrugs)*

Nobody knows what is going on kid. Maybe it's just a rumour. But then, maybe it is not.

RAJESH: *(Turning to Salim)*

Are they... are they supposed to be terrorists from across the border? Come here to kill us?

SALIM: *(Laughs)*

No. This time they are our own home-grown varieties trying to kill us.

RAJESH: *(Trembling)*

Musalman killing Hindus?

SALIM: And vice-versa. They are both killing each other and everybody else. That is called a communal riot and that is what is supposed to be happening out there.

(Rajesh looks at Salim for a long moment and then, frightened, moves to a straight chair and sits down hard.
Vikram watches him critically.
Reema has turned away.
Shanaz is leaning against the wall.
Jai moves towards him, pulls a chair next to him, sits down and pats him kindly on the arm.)

JAI: Don't panic, kid. It may not be true. It may just be a rumour after all, you know.

(Rajesh looks at him suspiciously)

RAJESH: Do you... do you mean it? Or are you saying it just to ...

(Stares at him for a moment, then looks at Salim and then takes out a cheap mobile from his pocket and fiddles with it for a while, then glances at the TV.)

JAI: No, the TV also has gone off the air; same time as the mobiles were jammed. It's just the Government ensuring that unfounded rumours don't spread around and make the situation worse. Don't let that worry you. Our Government is always doing something stupid like this.

RAJESH: *(Hesitantly)*

May be I should just go back –

JAI: Go back where, kid? And how will you get there? By the same back routes that you came here? Don't even try. Didn't you just hear that lady there
(Pointing at Reema)
say that the rumour is that there is a gang coming up the road and another down the road? Somewhere you will have to join the main road.

RAJESH: *(Nervously, trembling again)*

Are they both gangs of *Musalman*?

JAI: *(Shrugs)*

Who knows? Maybe they are and maybe

they are both Hindu gangs. Or maybe they are one of each. Listen to me; right now your best bet to keep safe is to stay put here. Most probably this talk of gangs on rampage is not true. And even if it is true, they won't find this resort, you know. It is way off from the main road and it is known as a Christian resort.

(Rajesh looks at him not totally convinced. Jai gives him an encouraging smile.)

JAI: Relax, kid. Nothing is going to happen to you or to anybody else here in this resort. Just sit tight in here until it is all over and then you can go home safely.
(Glances mischievously at Mathew.)
And Mathew here has got plenty of rooms for you to choose from. Even seven star ones with a view of the river.

(Mathew glowers at him.)

SHANAZ: Ask him if he can cook.

*(Reema laughs.
Salim guffaws.
Jai smothers a smile.
Rajesh looks around at all the faces feeling snubbed and a little humiliated, but the tension in him has visibly abated.)*

RAJESH: *(Turning to Jai, colouring)*

I... I haven't got any money to pay for a room.

VIKRAM: *(Looking disdainfully at Rajesh.)*

Doesn't the company give you any hotel allowance? I know they do. It's one of my companies that was supposed to be having this salesmen's convention at this time though I didn't know this was the place.

(Rajesh is startled, looks at him frightened and shrinks back.)

VIKRAM: And this is not a seven star hotel by a far chance. More suited to your allowance, I would say.

MATHEW: *(Staring pop-eyed at Vikram)*

One of your... your companies? Your... your company? You... you cancelled... you lost me my –

(Vikram turns and looks at Mathew. Mathew swallows. Vikram keeps on looking at him. Mathew reddens and looks down.)

MATHEW: N... n... nothing, Sir. Nothing.

(Vikram turns back to Rajesh.)

VIKRAM: *(Glaring at Rajesh)*

So?

RAJESH: *(Cowed down, not looking at Vikram)*

They... they do give; but... but... it gets spent on –

VIKRAM: *(Bullying him)*

Ah! So you cheat my company on hotel bills, do you? That's why you came the back way. You didn't take the sales route that was assigned to you, you didn't make the hotel stops you were supposed to make or you would have known that the convention was cancelled. And now you will present my company with false expense vouchers. You little scum!

RAJESH: *(Swallowing hard and looking up furtively)*

I... I... I mean... I don't really mean to cheat the company on the travelling expenses or anything like that, but... but... the instalment on the moped is pretty heavy and I don't really get much of a salary or commission and –

VIKRAM: *(Cutting him short)*

And you have a half-starved brood of children and a sick mother at home. Hah! Don't give me that sob story. I have heard it hundreds of times before from others in my other companies too. It is people like you who are bleeding us dry, making a mockery of our economic progress and –

(Jai raises a hand to cut Vikram short.)

JAI:

(To Rajesh, patting him on the arm)

It's ok kid. I understand what you are going through. You had no other recourse to make the ends meet. And I guess the ends are still wide apart while you watch your bosses live a life of luxury – seven star hotels and all that. It's not your fault. The fault lies with
(Looking at Vikram)
his company for not paying you a decent wage, for not caring enough for your welfare and thereby not inspiring you to do your best. You were only reacting to their treatment of you.
(To Vikram)
You pay third class wages, you don't get first class service; that's the rule of the world.

VIKRAM:

(Glaring at him)

You communists are all the same. You believe that only those who are low level workers have all the problems in the world and are therefore justified in cheating their employers. Did you stop to think that perhaps his pay is all that he is worth to my company? The way he is carrying on with his job, I would say my company is the loser in keeping him on.

JAI: Yeah? It is certainly making more than enough profit from his labour or it would have fired him a long time ago.

(Rajesh becomes terrified and looks pleadingly at Jai but doesn't dare to stop him.
Jai carries on to Vikram without noticing Rajesh's pleading look.)

I am sure your company is not a charity. In fact I am sure the managers and other bosses of your company are living very well indeed by exploiting him and a thousand more like him.

But then you wouldn't understand why he is forced to do what he does. You have never experienced a despairing lack of basic facilities with no means to alleviate it. You have never had sleepless nights wondering where your next meal is coming from.

Only those who have to struggle to eat know what hunger means. And only those who suffer understand the meaning of pain.

VIKRAM: Ah, so you think that those of us in the managerial capacity wallow in a parasitical life of pomp and luxury because of his labour and that of thousands like him and have no worries, no cares of any sort, do you? You forget that if it wasn't for my company, he wouldn't have a job at all. It is people like me, people with initiative, who are carrying the load of providing employment to him and thousands more like him on our shoulders. Do you realise that if I were to just languish around in pomp and luxury, if I were to default in my responsibility to my companies, I would be ruining the lives of thousands of families? You ever think that? You ever think that these concerns wouldn't weigh heavy on me? That they wouldn't give me sleepless nights?

REEMA: *(To Jai)*

And don't forget the other concerns that he has, the more important ones, ones that really keep him awake all night, tossing and turning in his bed. Worries like for his low golf scores, the tick that his favourite Mercedes has developed and whether there is any French wine in the bar for the Government Minister who is coming for dinner the next night.

*(Vikram turns his glare on her.
Reema ignores him.)*

REEMA: *(Still addressing Jai)*

You shouldn't mind him, Jai. He is just in a bad mood because he is missing his evening aperitif. There is no mini-bar in our room, or even a bar down here, you see.

MATHEW: I have a few bottles – unofficially, of course – hidden in my desk. I applied for a liquor license but –

VIKRAM: *(Talking over Mathew, blowing up at Reema)*

It's easy for you to say! Rich man's rich daughter! Your life has been one of shopping, clubs and dancing. What do you know about the stress of running the factories, of managing the business or anything about the tea estates? Or about how I have to stay on my toes all the time watching out for the problems that may crop up anywhere in any of these and nipping them in the bud before they engulf everything? Or about how I have to deal with the politicians and the licensing authorities and the export officials to ensure that they don't create some stupid obstacles? Yes, I have to flaunt a Mercedes to impress the right people and play golf with them because all the important deals are made on the golf course. And yes, I have to entertain the Government Ministers in style. Do you realise what would happen to all these enterprises if they all weren't kept happy? What do you know about how much I have to exert to keep everything moving smoothly? What do you know of my struggles? Did you ever even care to know?

(Blackout for a moment.
Then only the footlights on the balcony come on to

shine upwards on Vikram standing on the balcony.
In the shadowy light on the rest of the stage all others
stay stock-still maintaining their positions.)

VIKRAM:

What does she know of my struggles – my struggles of now or before; of what my life had been before all this? What does anybody know of that time of watching my inferiors being promoted all the time, the frustration of waiting around doing some lowly, ill-paid work knowing, knowing all the time that I was capable of attaining much more, of doing much better?

And I have proved myself. I have expanded all those interests – the factories, the businesses, though it did entail a lot of hard toil, some ruthless measures, keeping tabs on the market, on demands, on competitors, managing all the authorities – it has not been easy to reach where I have reached. But I have.

And who was there to share my worries, to take some load off my shoulders, to provide me with some succour? My father-in-law who thought I was getting into areas beyond my capabilities, who always cautioned me to hold back, hold back, not jump into the big pool? A wife who disdained me because of my background, who was never there for me, who ignored my existence and lived her own separate life?

(Hesitantly, in a low voice)

I have achieved a lot, I have made my mark in this world of commerce, I am looked up to by others and yet I don't feel secure. I still lie awake at nights and I toss and turn in my bed at the thought of losing it all. I am afraid to go to sleep in the fear that I will wake up in the morning and find it has all been a dream, that I am still an ill-paid low level worker that I was.

Yes, I have spent sleepless nights; yes, I have toiled; but I *have* created an empire.

(In a pained voice, throwing his hands out)

But of what use is an empire if there is no one to inherit it?

(Blackout for a moment.

Then lights come on as before and all are in same positions as before.)

VIKRAM: *(To Reema, aggressively)*

Yes, I have sleepless nights. Yes I toss and turn in my bed all night. You know why? Because *I* was the one who took your father's businesses into an area that your father had never even dreamed of. It was *I* who brought them into national limelight, you understand? And now *I* have to struggle not only to maintain that position but to climb still further. Given time *I* can take them into the A-1 list of companies. And all these responsibilities and worries lie on *my* shoulders, and *mine* alone. That's what keeps me awake at night, you understand?

(Pushing his face into hers)

YOU UNDERSTAND?

REEMA: *(Coldly)*

You are making a fool of yourself, Vikram.

(Vikram flinches, then gets up and goes to stand by the sideboard looking into distance.
Salim turns to the window.
Rajesh has been looking in a terrified manner from one to another and now shrinks further into himself searching for a corner to hide in.
All others are consciously looking away from Vikram trying to hide their embarrassment.
Jai gets up, goes to stand by Shanaz and rests a hand in a relaxed manner on the wall that Shanaz is leaning against.)

JAI: *(To Shanaz in an effort to divert everybody's attention and lighten the atmosphere)*

That was quite a dance, Shanaz. Where did you learn it? Is that how you danced in the bar? I have never been to one, you see. We don't have them where I work; but then even our people in cities are not expected to spend their time and their money in dance bars. They are supposed to be serious about our cause, not be given to being frivolous.

SHANAZ: *(Snorts)*

You will be surprised to know how many of you communists used to come to the bar; and how much money they threw about on the girls. Where do they get it from? I always thought all the communists were poor. They always move around in kurta-pyjamas, like you. And distribute hand-bills at the street corners during the day.

JAI: *(Laughing patronisingly)*

How did you know those in your bar were communists? Not everybody in a kurta-pyjama is a communist, Shanaz. And is that all you know of communists? That they move about in kurta-pyjamas? And distribute hand-bills?

SHANAZ: They also have those sit-ins in all the squares and also those hours-long marches on the streets holding those placards over their heads and shouting slogans when they block all the traffic and make it difficult for us to go anywhere. Don't they ever think of us poor people who have to stand for hours in a queue for a bus and then the bus gets stuck in a traffic jam because of their rally and doesn't move at all? Don't they have any work to do?

SALIM: *(Turning around and laughing)*

That is their work, Shanaz. They are working to improve the lives of those same poor people who have to wait hours for a bus.

(Shanaz looks uncertainly at Salim and then laughs.)

SHANAZ: *That* is work? And they get *paid* for it? Who pays them for *that* work?

(Salim looks at her impressed.
Jai straightens up looking annoyed.)

SALIM: The people, Shanaz. It's always the people who pay, directly or indirectly. People like you and Rajesh over there.

(Rajesh looks up at the mention of his name.)

SHANAZ: *(Pointing at Vikram)*

And him?

SALIM: *(Shaking his head)*

No, not him. People like him never pay. They collect.

(Vikram looks daggers at him.)

JAI: *(To Salim, still aggravated)*

Well, why shouldn't the people pay for them if they are working to improve the lot of the same people?
(To Shanaz, seriously)
That's right, Shanaz. They *are* striving for

the betterment of the working people, to improve the quality of their lives. People like you, so that you don't have to wait hours for a bus or dance in a bar anymore but can live a dignified life.

SHANAZ: *(Pouting)*

But I liked working in the bar. I liked dancing. And I liked people throwing money at me. It was good money. I could live well. I was my own mistress. I could do what I wanted, make my own decisions and didn't have to depend on anybody's moods or charity.
And what would I have done if I didn't work in a bar?
(Angrily)
The same thing that I did after the bar closed? Be at his
(Points at Vikram)
beck and call? Pander to his wants and likes and dislikes and vices? Lie about everything, agree with everything he says and do whatever he asks me to do even if I hate it? You think that is any better?

(Vikram looks at her startled.)

SHANAZ: *(Still angrily)*

Or you think it is better to work as a maid, sweep and mop other people's houses all day long?

(Jai looks at her nonplussed.
Salim looks at her with understanding.)

JAI: *(Persisting)*

But don't you want a home and a family of your own? What did you do before you started dancing in that bar? How long have you been dancing in there? Didn't your family mind it? Wouldn't you like to go back home again?

SHANAZ: *(Looks at him with pure hatred.)*

Do I want a home and family? You call it a home? Ever lived in a slum, all seven of you in one room? Ever fought over water at a single dripping tap and then come back to your room with just half a pot of water for the whole family's needs? You think it is any fun living with that all-pervading stink and noise and with no privacy at all?

(Blackout for a moment.
Then only the footlights on the balcony come on to shine upwards on Shanaz standing on the balcony.
In the shadowy light on the rest of the stage, all others stay stock-still maintaining their positions.)

SHANAZ: What did I do before? He should have asked me what all had happened to me and how I have still managed to make a life for myself.

What a life it has been! Taken out of the school at a young age, married, divorced, made to work for my living, raped and knifed in a riot. Having to act as a willing vessel because some patron wanted a son and his wife was sterile. All at some man's will.

(Pause)

A long time ago, after my divorce, I had to find some work. My brother had made it clear to me. First I did some sweeping and mopping in people's houses and then found a job as a nursing assistant in a nursing home. The nursing home where I worked was no great shakes; nor was the pay; but the patients who came there treated me with respect for the extra help I gave them, even gratitude for the small tasks I did for them. And I got over my feelings of inferiority, of always having to be subservient to some man – father, husband, brother – for the food that he spared for me, for the clothes he bought for me. A very long time ago.

Then came the riots. Now my family is mostly gone and those who are living don't want to know me because I am tainted. I have been raped by the kafirs. Was that my fault?

My fault was that I accepted the taint, I hid in shame. The shame of the victim. I couldn't get rid of that feeling of guilt, and the helplessness, servility and the meekness that I had developed again.

Alone and destitute, I accepted that job in the bar because there was no other alternative.

But strangely, I enjoyed dancing in that bar. In dance I could forget everything that pained me: my childhood, my marriage, the riot. From childhood I had always loved to dance but there was nowhere to dance where the family and other people did not stare at me oddly and fearfully and then hurriedly forced me to stop. In the bar I was encouraged to dance. I was in demand. And there I also realised the power that I had over men. One glance from under my eyelashes and they were ready to lick my feet. I could wrap them around my little finger like this slip of a salesman or even the Sahib. I had always been in some man's power and so now I enjoyed the power I exerted over men.

But there was another side to it also, not altogether pleasant. Though I danced for myself, those lecherous, salivating looks could not be avoided. They raped me physically when I didn't dance and with their eyes when I danced. So I used my power over them, I used my body to make them dance to my tune, but I still hated them all. Hated them and feared them.

(Pause)

Then the bar closed and the savings didn't last long. We had lived high. I was afraid to walk the streets like many other girls did but one has to survive. When Sahib came along I thought I was lucky; but he also demanded the same age-old servility, the same humility and the same submissiveness from me. And now Jai lectures me on the right way to live!

(Pause)

Why do men always try to fit us in the mould they have in their minds for us: a docile woman; a sexual object; a housewife?

Except for Salim. Salim doesn't lecture me, doesn't expect me to change myself, doesn't expect anything else from me except that I pretend to be his wife. He listens to me; and he lets me be myself. And his money will make me independent of all men. I will not take any nonsense from anyone anymore. Now, I will do and speak exactly as I feel; and I couldn't care less who doesn't like it.

Strange, how money in one's pocket translates into power in one's mind.

(Blackout for a moment.
Then lights come on as before and all are in same positions as before.)

SHANAZ: *(To Jai, still angrily)*

You think a slum is a paradise? Do you know what those girls in the slums dream about? I will tell you. They don't dream about a home in a slum and having to manage a family on a pittance. They dream about wearing the sort of clothes I wore while dancing in the bar and they dream that a Shah Rukh Khan or a Hrithik Roshan will come and carry them away into the rising sun in a long white car, just like in the movies. And what they get is shopping for second-hand clothes at the roadside stalls and a drunkard truck driver for a husband who swears at them and beats them and then leaves them holding a howling brood of kids.

So don't ask me what I did before and whether I want a home and family or not. It's none of your business.

(Goes off in a huff and sits next to Rajesh.
Rajesh smiles shyly at her.
Jai looks at her stumped.
Pause)

MATHEW: *(Brightly)*

Would anybody like to play cards?

(Looks around at everybody with a bright smile.
Jai turns his angry look on him.
Reema looks haughtily back at him,
Vikram disgustedly.
Shanaz and Rajesh look confused,
non-understanding.
Salim laughs.)

CURTAIN

ACT III

(Later same night.
A single light focuses on the clock on the wall.
The clock shows and tolls 10.00 p.m.
Light on the clock fades out on the last peal of the clock.
A dim light comes on to light the stage.
Relaxed atmosphere in the room.
Mathew is sitting on a hard chair at the sideboard with a ledger spread before him.
Vikram is sitting in the sofa chair apart from others reading a newspaper.
Reema and Jai are sitting together on the sofa talking.
Salim is standing by the window singing softly.
Rajesh and Shanaz are sitting together on hard chairs – in the opposite corner from Vikram – bending over the catalogues that Rajesh is showing to Shanaz.
A single bright light comes on and moves from person to person as they talk.
Others who are in the dim light stay still until the light shines on them.
Light shines on Rajesh and Shanaz.)

RAJESH: No, No, it is a blusher. It comes with a little
                  soft brush. You have to put it on your cheeks
                  to make them red.

SHANAZ: *(Interested)*

And this green colour? What is that for?

RAJESH: That is an eye-shadow. You put it on your
                   eyelids. You don't use it?

SHANAZ: *(Laughs)*

                   That will make me look like a joker.
                   *(Giving him an inviting glance and fluttering
                   her eyelashes)*
                   I use only powder, kajal and lipstick.

RAJESH: *(Enchanted)*

                   You really don't need anything more but
                   a blue eye-shadow will look very good
                   on you.
                   (Looking at her shyly)
                   You dance very well.

SHANAZ: *(Coldly)*

                   I don't dance any more.
                   (Suddenly brightens up)
                   Now I am going to get lots of money and I
                   am going to do something quite different.
                   (Looks naughtily at Rajesh.)
                   May be I will sell things like you?
                   (Imitating Rajesh)
                   'Would you like a green eye-shadow Madam,
                   to make you look like a joker?'

                   (Laughs.

Rajesh looks at her perplexed, then reddens and looks down.

Shanaz turns away from him, puts her elbow on the palm of the other hand and supports her chin on her hand thinking.

Light moves to shine on Shanaz alone.

Shanaz's voice-over is heard in the background.)

SHANAZ'S
VOICE-OVER:

I will do something different. No more any of those nursing home or other jobs – not that anybody will hire me now with my background. And I will never go back to being a kept woman. No more servility now.

I would have liked to go back to dancing. Could I join some class to learn proper dancing? And then join a group that gives public performances? I guess it is too late for that.

Then what shall I do? I will have money to invest now.

Maybe I will start a business. Some girls I know have done that. They have a small cubicle shop and they sell gilt jewellery and knick-knacks. But you have to be good at reading the clients' faces, they tell me. You look at their clothes and their eyes and flatter them and then fix your price accordingly. I would be good at that after all the practice I have had. Maybe I will join them.

And maybe someday I will meet some nice guy who will love me for myself and we will get married and live happily ever after. What a fairy tale that will be!

(Light moves to include Rajesh.
Shanaz laughs to herself and then turns and
smiles brightly at Rajesh.)

SHANAZ: I am going to bécome a businesswoman,
                 Rajesh.

                 (Rajesh looks at her bewildered.
                 Pause
                 Light moves on to Mathew.
                 Mathew lays down his pen and sighs.)

MATHEW: *(Shaking his head in exasperation, to himself)*

                 Expenses, expenses, expenses. And not
                 much income.

                 (Sighs)

                 What a devil of a day it has been.

                 (Sighs again, sits back and looks up, pensive.
                 Mathew's voice-over is heard in background.)

MATHEW'S
VOICE-OVER: What a day it has been. The high when
                 that marketing company booked the whole
                 resort. The low when they cancelled it. But
                 then a rich couple frightened of a rumour
                 came to stay in the most expensive room and
                 gave me an idea.
                 Now I have to attract a better class of clients.
                 No more of those travelling salesmen and
                 the clerks and small businessmen who have

patronised my resort up to now. Only classy people; real classy.

I should put up a billboard at the junction of the highway. And print some colourful posters and stick them at the railway station – no! It is the car-owners that I really want to attract, not the lowly clientele that has to travel on trains and buses. So where else can I advertise? Ah! At the petrol stations!

And I have to learn to say 'sir' and 'madam' more often. And I have to learn to be more obsequious. Rich people everywhere expect it – like this couple here. And I have to find ways of charging them extras. Small things, like flowers and fruit. Offer them some gracious little things and then charge them outrageously.

But first of all, I must make a special offering in the church when I go to the mass this Sunday to thank the Almighty for leading this couple to my resort.

(Mathew grins happily.)

Good!

(Mathew turns back to his ledger.
Pause
Light moves on to Vikram.
Vikram turns a page of the newspaper.)

VIKRAM: *(Loudly. To the room in general)*

All the news is about the possibility of countrywide riots, but nothing conclusive.

There are many opinions – all contradictory to each other of course. As expected. Some say now it is an unavoidable certainty and others say that it can still be curbed.

(Disgustedly)

The editorial is noncommittal as usual.

(Looks up from the paper thinking.
Vikram's voice-over is heard in the background.)

VIKRAM'S
VOICE-OVER:

I had better watch out in the factories. That's where the future problems can start – not in businesses or on tea estates. There have already been some signs of tensions, some discontent. I don't want the police to be called in again. They also need to be gratified. Or I have to call in a favour. But every favour also needs to be returned.

To begin with I had better segregate the labour force in the factory – community-wise – to forestall any possible friction and the resulting problems. Put them in totally separate units despite their abilities and inclinations in one field or other. They will just have to learn to adjust; or else.

(Vikram looks satisfied, then shifts his attention to the newspaper again and turns a page)

VIKRAM:

(Loudly. To the room in general.)

Sensex has gone down again.

(Pause
Light moves onto Reema and Jai.
Reema glances at Vikram and turns back to Jai.)

JAI: *(Looking at Salim)*

He has gone back to being his old self, hasn't he? The same old Salim: always laughing, disrespectful of all politics, dismissive of all the isms, always an optimistic singer. And to think that all this time that I have been here, he had been unbearably cold and stony. Forget about a laugh, not even a proper smile out of him; more of a cold sneer. Very unlike his old self.
(Looks meditatively at Reema.)
He has aged though, hasn't he? Aged far beyond his years. There is pain and coldness in his eyes where there used to be only laughter and warmth.

REEMA: So have you Jai.

JAI: So have you, you know Reema. I guess it has not been too easy on you either.
Do you remember those days, Reema, once, long ago, when we were young? How carefree we were. Everything was going to work out for us exactly as we wanted it to. How easy it had seemed then to be able to change the world to what we wanted it to be.
(Sadly)

The world is still the same; it has only changed us. And I am not sure it is for the better.

(Reema looks down at her hands sadly and dejectedly for a moment and then turns to Jai with a bright, artificial smile.)

REEMA: Can I visit you in the jungle, Jai?

JAI: *(Smiles at her)*

Of course. Any time you like. Just let me know beforehand and I will send the limousine to pick you up. And also let me know what you would like for dinner. The choice in our wine cellar is rather limited, I am afraid.

(Reema raps him on the knuckles)

REEMA: I am serious, Jai. Since I am going to go back into investigative journalism, what better introductory piece than a story from inside a Naxalite hideout? And not just a piece on what you all wear and eat and where you sleep and how much you walk every day, etcetera, but a real in-depth study of the reasons behind it all and reactions to it; not from your city-bred, dyed-in-the-wool communists but from the local recruits, the tribals. What do they all in those camps believe in, what do they expect the end results to be, whether they have any qualms about an armed revolution, you know, things like that.

Let me start with you, Jai, what do you think of this reign of terror that the Naxalites have unleashed? I still refuse to believe that *you* are a willing party to it.
Hold on.

(Finds and opens her handbag and fumbles for a pen. Then sorts out the papers in the bag, takes out a bill, looks at it and chooses the reverse side of it. She rests the paper on her bag and looks expectantly at Jai.)

JAI: *(Suddenly looking serious and tired, all his playfulness gone)*

No, terror can't solve any problems. It is only reversal of power roles between the parties. Yet it is very complex, Reema. If you saw the plight of the tribals, you also would pick up arms on their behalf. I am not telling you anything new. They have been cruelly oppressed now for tens of centuries and everybody exploits those who are without power to retaliate.
I will take you around some of the tribal areas when you come, Reema. The forests are going; their land is being eroded beyond any recovery; they can hardly grow enough to eat. And with the new mines and big dams being licensed on their lands and forests all the time, what are they supposed to do? Where do they go? And when they protest, the police come. With their guns.

More burnings, beatings, rapes and killings. The callousness of it all is enough to chill your blood.

You should see the havoc the mine owners have rendered on the land there, the scorched earth that they have left behind. What future are they leaving for our children, Reema?

I read somewhere that the super-rich have already started buying plots on the moon and are booking their seats on the space shuttle for abandoning the earth when it becomes unliveable. And I laughed, thinking, well, well! even they are gullible enough to be taken in by some enterprising scamsters. And then I read that some scientists are also preparing to pack their geodesic domes and join the exodus and I sat up. You can understand what it means, Reema, if the scientists too believe that the earth is bound to become unliveable; and that too in the near enough future. I wonder sometimes if we are just doing a Band-aid treatment on a dying patient.

(Jai smiles a weary smile.

Reema has stopped writing and is staring at him.)

We took a protest march of twenty-five thousand tribals to Delhi. Did we get a peep out of anybody? Not only the Government but even the media and the public totally ignored us. The only people who paid any attention to us were the police – asking us to get off the road, not hold up the traffic, not make so much noise. Peaceful social activists are being victimised every day. So what other recourse do any of us have left except taking up arms? Violence is necessary in certain situations, Reema; not only necessary but unavoidable. But violence has to be selective in the object of its impact, for a particular purpose and aimed at a definite achievement.

That is where the problem lies Reema, in knowing how to organise, how to control and how to direct this revolt towards a constructive end, not just towards a maliciously destructive one. And I don't think we have been able to do that. Most of the recruits – and some of them, yes, are forced recruits – have no inkling of any ideology, as you will see when you visit the camp. And this power of the gun goes to their heads – especially when they have been powerless for so long. If you don't give it a proper direction, then you land up with a reign of terror.

(Pause)

But where we have liberated the areas from the landlords, the police, the forest officers and where the mining lords don't dare step, we have done some other things too Reema. We have organised them into a cohesive unit. We have brought in agricultural and horticultural experts and started water conservation, rejuvenation of the dead soil and forest cultivation again.

REEMA: But I have also read that Naxalites too are taking the tribals for a ride. That they also go on a killing, looting spree, even in tribal areas. And if development is their aim, then how come that they are the ones who close schools and hospitals and blow up the roads and bridges while facilitating mining companies for underhand cash?

JAI: *(Sighs wearily)*

It's not utopia there, Reema.
But don't make the mistake of believing that the tribals are all good, simple, childlike people or noble and naïve; or of equating poverty with honesty and decency. You will find patriarchy and chauvinism, greed and cruelty and dictatorial, exploitative tendencies not only among the police but also among the tribals and also among the Naxalites. The self-serving instinct is equally strong in all of us, Reema.

REEMA: *(Soberly)*

What does the future look like, Jai?

JAI: *(Frowning.)*

Bleak, Reema, very bleak. The tribals have had a taste of power now. They won't easily give in to –

(Sound of a car stopping outside.

All the lights on the stage come on.
Everybody tenses and looks towards left archway.
Knocking is heard on unseen door left.)

VOICE CALLING
FROM OUTSIDE: Open   up   for   Deviji,   Minister   in
the Government.

(Mathew looks at everybody a little confused.
Rajesh and Shanaz also look confused.
Vikram looks up hopefully.
Reema raises her eyebrows.
Jai and Salim become alert.
Salim's hand goes to his waistband.
Jai quickly gets up and goes to the left window and
looks out.)

JAI: It *is* Deviji. But when did she become a
Minister in the Government? She was in the
opposition party.

VIKRAM: She changed the party when this ministerial
position was offered to her.

JAI: *(With a sardonic smile)*

Of course. One party is the same as all the
others after all, with the same agenda – that
of promoting self-interest of its members at
any cost.

(Vikram frowns at him.
Jai glances at Salim and then at the rear door but
doesn't move.

Mathew looks at him and then, as the knocking repeats, goes through the left archway.
Sounds of bolts being drawn are heard.
Mathew backs onto the stage holding his hands above his head followed by a black-cat security guard training a gun on him.
The backs of Mathew's legs touch the sofa and he flops down on it still holding his hands high.
The security guard sweeps the room with the gun and then turns his gun on each of them individually giving each a hard stare and then satisfied, holsters his gun and speaks into his walkie-talkie.
Mathew lowers his hands with a sigh of relief.
Deviji enters followed by her secretary carrying another walkie-talkie and a pad and pen.
The security guard looks up the stairs, pulls out his gun again and runs upstairs.
Deviji bows left and right with her hands joined in namaskar.
Vikram stands up and bows with joined hands.
No response from anyone else. They all stare at her dumbly.)

DEVIJI: *(In a monotone)*

Namaste, Namaste. Don't get up, don't up, sit down, sit down.

(Nobody else has moved. Those sitting are still sitting. Vikram lowers his hands but keeps standing and then glances at Reema raising his eyebrows and flicking his chin up as if asking her to stand up also.

Reema doesn't move.
Deviji doesn't seem to notice. She holds her hands up, palms outside, and continues in the same monotone.)

DEVIJI: We are going through a difficult time. At a time like this, people should be brave and courageous, should behave and act sensibly. Do not believe in any wild rumours. Do not act rashly. There is nothing to worry about. We have the situation well under control. We are responding in an organised manner. All appropriate measures are in progress and all necessary steps have been taken. The Chief Minister has also visited the Vishnu temple and performed a Maha Puja there for peace. So there is no reason to panic. Do not give in to sensationalisation of the news. Keep calm. Keep calm.

(Stops and looks around vaguely and then glances towards the stairs.
Vikram advances towards her with his hands joined together and bows to her again.
The secretary moves to block him but Deviji looks Vikram over in a speculative manner and stays the secretary with a flick of her hand.)

VIKRAM: Namaste Deviji. I am Vikram Dixit. You may remember I had met you once before, during that meeting of the industrialists that you had called?

(Deviji glances at the secretary.
He nods.)

DEVIJI: Yes, yes, of course. I hope all your problems were solved in that meeting. We did take a note of all your recommendations. But if you still have any problems, come and see me in the office. Just make an appointment through my secretary here on his cell phone. We will see what we can do. We can't let our country's development be hampered by some small glitches and industries are the backbone of our country. Rules and regulations are meant to be applied judiciously.
(To the secretary)
Give him your card.

(The secretary delves in his pocket and gives a card to Vikram.
Vikram looks at it, puts it in his pocket and turns to Deviji again.)

VIKRAM: You are always gracious, Deviji. I certainly will come and meet you. It's the understanding and the unflinching assistance given by you that is making the industry take great leaps forward.

(The security guard comes down again.
Deviji turns to look at him.
Vikram glances at him and turns back to Deviji.)

VIKRAM: I was wondering if I could impose a little on your kindness –

DEVIJI: *(Looks questioningly at the security guard while talking off-handedly to Vikram)*

Yes, yes, of course. Just make an appointment and come to my office.

SECURITY
GUARD: It's quite safe here, Deviji. I think you should come upstairs and rest a little before the helicopter arrives.

VIKRAM: *(Hurriedly)*

You see I and my wife are stranded here because of –

(The secretary interrupts Vikram by putting up his hand and gestures to Deviji to move towards the stairs while blocking Vikram with his arm.)

SECRETARY: *(To Vikram)*

It has been a very tense time for Deviji what with all those hectic meetings and then this mad rush to get out of the area on getting that urgent message. She has been on her feet all day but she will still spend time soothing people, like now. She works too hard. She must take some rest now.

*(Vikram steps back.
Deviji has moved to the stairs but stops at the bottom of it and turns to face them.)*

DEVIJI: I will do anything for my people, I will suffer anything for them. We are here only to serve the people.

(Deviji goes up the stairs followed by the security guard and watched silently by all.
The security guard stops on the landing and leans over the handrail.)

SECURITY
GUARD: *(To the secretary)*

             Where did that escorting police jeep go to?

SECRETARY: To survey the situation around.

SECURITY
GUARD: Well, check with them, will you?

             (Goes through the archway on the landing)

MATHEW: *(To Vikram)*

             See, I told you they were all rumours.

JAI: Then why is she in such a great hurry to leave this area? Calling a helicopter to pick her up and all that?
             (Sarcastically)
             Anyway the Chief Minister has performed a Maha Puja at the Vishnu temple so everything is taken care of. We can all relax now. We have nothing to worry about.

(Rajesh nervously approaches the secretary.)

RAJESH: *(Anxiously)*

It is true, isn't it? What the Lady Minister said? That they are all only rumours?

SECRETARY: *(Gives a half smile while punching his walkie-talkie and speaks without looking up.)*

You heard her.

(Rajesh moves back uncertainly.
Vikram keeps standing where he is.
The secretary keeps punching his walkie-talkie.
Everybody waits apprehensively, glancing up the stairs every now and then.
The security guard comes out of the upper archway and stands on the landing watching everybody.)

SECURITY
GUARD: *(To the secretary)*

Are you sure the helicopter will come here?

SECRETARY: Of course it will. I gave the pilot this exact location as soon as we heard of those two armed mobs – one coming up the road and the other coming down the road – just before my mobile went off the air. I knew of this Christian resort, the only in-between place that is also a bit off the highway.

(Suddenly everybody becomes alert and sits up.
Mathew's mouth drops open.
The secretary's walkie-talkie rings. He answers,
listens, disconnects.)

SECRETARY: *(To the security guard)*

The police say better hurry up. Those two mobs are advancing on the highway. May reach here quite soon now unless they veer off the highway towards some villages on the way. And the police also say that both the mobs are very violent and they won't be able to stop or even hinder those mobs in any way.

SECURITY
GUARD: *(Anxiously)*

Where is that damn helicopter? It should have been here by now. It wasn't too far off when you called it.

(Runs down the stairs and goes to the window.
Everybody has tensed up now.)

RAJESH: So it's true. It's true they are coming up and down the road.

(He rushes to the secretary.
Vikram tugs his sleeves down and also approaches the secretary.
Shanaz moves in behind them.)

120

RAJESH: Listen, listen, take me with you.

                    (The secretary doesn't even look at him. He is busy scribbling on his pad.)

RAJESH: *(Tentatively touching the secretary's sleeve, in a pleading voice)*

                    Take me with you, please, please, take me with you. I have got old parents and a sister to be married and brothers who are still in school and –

                    (The secretary doesn't respond. Rajesh panics.)

RAJESH: *(Agitated)*

                    Please, don't leave me here, please. They will kill me. Those *Musalman*s will kill me –

                    (Vikram stands straight and holds the secretary's arm to make him look up.)

VIKRAM: You heard Deviji. I am important to our country's development. You can't leave *me* here at the mercy of those thugs. You will be hindering the progress of our country –

                    (Mathew jumps up and grabs the security guard's arm.)

MATHEW: You can't leave here. You have to stay and protect us, protect this resort. That's your duty. You can't go, you can't just go and leave my resort at the mercy of those gangs. Where is that police jeep? Why aren't they here to protect us?

(The security guard shakes Mathew's hand off his arm and pushes him away. Mathew lands open-mouthed on the sofa.

Sound of a helicopter arriving outside.
A strong floodlight shines through the window.

Everybody freezes staring out of the window.
The security guard glances out of the window and then moves to the centre of the room, takes out his gun and points it at them.)

SECURITY
GUARD: *(To the secretary)*

Get Deviji.

(The secretary breaks free of Rajesh and Vikram and runs up the stairs and then comes down again following Deviji and starts pushing her towards left archway.
The security guard is sweeping the room with his gun as he follows them backwards.
Deviji stops halfway to the archway.)

DEVIJI: *(Turning to them and joining her hands again.)*

Namaste. Keep calm, keep calm. Everything

is under control. And be assured that we will not be intimidated; we will not give in to any blackmail. The whole police force is out there with all their personnel. And the Home Minister has also sent the army in. We will also call in National Security Guards and Elite Forces if necessary. Air Force is also on the alert. The Home Minister has the situation well assessed. So keep calm, keep calm. There is nothing to worry about. Namaste, Namaste.

(Rajesh and Vikram, who are still standing, crowd Deviji.
Mathew runs over to her.
Shanaz is standing behind them.
Salim and Reema haven't moved.
Jai is watching alertly.)

RAJESH: *(In desperation)*

Please take me with you, take me with you. Please, please, please. Don't leave me here, please, don't–

MATHEW: The police, the police. You said the police will protect –

VIKRAM: *(Trying to move in front of Deviji)*

Deviji –

(Deviji looks at him and then looks at the secretary raising her eyebrows questioningly.

The secretary shakes his head imperceptibly.)

SECRETARY: *(Whispers)*

Not on A-1 list.

(Vikram flinches.
The secretary tries to push them all back while Deviji tries to sidestep them.
Jai joins the melee.)

JAI: At least take the women with you. Surely your helicopter is big enough to accommodate just the two of them.

(The security guard pushes Deviji to one side and points his gun at them.
They fall back.
Deviji and the secretary exit.
The security guard backs out last still waving his gun at them at arm's length, leaving them standing numb, mouths open.
Barrel of the gun is the last to vanish behind the archway.
Sound of helicopter leaving.
Floodlight shining through the window goes off.
Rajesh and Vikram are standing stupefied.
Shanaz has retreated to stand leaning against a wall.
Mathew flops down on the sofa.
Rajesh; dazed, numbly goes and sits on a chair.)

RAJESH: She doesn't really care, does she? She doesn't care for people at all.

(Nobody pays any attention to him.
Jai glances at him and then joins Salim at
the window.
Both are looking grim.)

JAI: Did you hear her? Be brave and courageous? We won't give in to blackmail? What the heck does that mean? And they will call National Security Guards and Elite Forces? To control a rioting crowd? What is she talking about?

SALIM: What were *you* thinking about Jai, begging and pleading with her like that? Did you really expect any help from her? Didn't you just now spout about how those with advantages never help those who are without them? How the powerful only want to help themselves?

JAI: The fact is that the Home Minister has sent the army in. Against our own people! You understand what *that* means. That the police force cannot control this situation by itself.

SALIM: *(Nods)*

That also means that they are mobs; not just gangs out there on the streets but mobs! Not in tens or hundreds but in thousands. And also that these riots *are* widespread, all over the country.

(They stare silently at each other for a long moment.)

VIKRAM: *(Going to Mathew and pointing a finger at him)*

                     Rumours, you said. Rumours! Hah! Safe over
                     here, you said. Safe, hah!

MATHEW: *(Babbling)*

                     They won't come here, I told you. They
                     will go on the highway. They will pass us
                     by. They *can't* come here. They *can't* loot
                     what I have created with so much effort. The
                     police will protect us. The Home Minister
                     promised... Deviji also said the whole
                     police force ...
                     (Suddenly remembering)
                     That police jeep. That police jeep will come
                     back. They will protect us. She said the whole
                     police force will protect us.

VIKRAM: *(Throwing his arms up.)*

                     Hah! Didn't you hear that secretary say that
                     the police can't stop or even hinder those
                     mobs? They have most surely already slunk
                     away trying to save their own skins. The
                     whole police force! Against the murdering
                     mobs? Hah!

                     (Goes and stands by the sideboard.)

MATHEW: My resort, my resort, they can't loot my resort.
                     *(Gets up and moves around touching paintings
                     and curios.)*

Not my resort!

(Blackout for a moment.
Then only the footlights on the balcony come on to
shine upwards on Mathew standing on the balcony.
In the shadowy light on the rest of the stage, all
others stay stock-still maintaining their positions.)

MATHEW: My resort. All my life I have struggled and
struggled to acquire this property, to start
my own resort. Resort! Actually it is just a
small-little hotel with a couple of cottages,
some rooms and a few facilities that goes by
the grandiose name of resort. Cheaply built,
cheaply furnished. But it is mine. I skimped
and saved, begged and borrowed from all
and everybody, and I have made it a reality.
And now they are coming here to loot it!
Why are they coming here? Why have they
been attacking us Christians? What have
they got against us? We Christians are so
meek. We never make any demands. We
don't march, we don't organise strikes. We
never take any positions in politics; we don't
even have our own political party. We are
not aggressive like the Muslims. We don't
parade our religion like the Hindus. We
are not big entrepreneurs exploiting others
for our profits. We just go to church every
Sunday and mind our own business. All we
want is to be left alone to manage our small-
little businesses, to make our living. That
is all.

I have always been a good Christian – ever since my childhood when I used to go to the Sunday School and learned to follow its precepts. That is what my mother had taught me to do and I have religiously followed it. I have always attended the mass on Sundays. And I have always confessed all that I felt I had done wrong. And then faithfully performed the penance that the Father Confessor gave me. I have regularly contributed to the church collection. And I have explicitly put my trust in the Almighty God that He will make everything come right for me as He deems right.

He knows what all I have gone through to start this resort and what it means to me. He knows. He will not let them loot or destroy what I have mortgaged my soul for. He will not. He will protect my resort.

No, they will not come here. They will go on the highway. They will not loot my paintings, my silver, my curios – I spent days and days in the old markets searching for them –

And I just got new windows put in – with coloured glass. And I put in a new staircase railing –

(Stops suddenly and stands straight.)

I have got to hide them. God helps those who help themselves, that's what the Father at the church had said. I have got to hide whatever can be looted. When they find that there is nothing much to loot over here, then they will just leave.

(Blackout for a moment.
Then lights come on as before and all are in same
positions as before.)

MATHEW: *(Looking around)*

The store room. I have to lock it all up in the
store room.
(Hurriedly collects a handful of curios, stuffs a
couple of cushions under his arm and then stops
looking at the windows.)
They can't take the windows or the staircase
with them.

(Rushes out through the right archway.
Vikram goes and sits on the sofa exactly like
Mathew in the place vacated by him.)

VIKRAM: *(To no one in particular)*

So they are coming. Is that so? So we
are all going to be killed. Damn these
bloody Muslims!

(Reema has got up and is moving around like a
caged animal – obviously on edge – seemingly
ready to blow up at anybody for anything and
rounds on Vikram.)

REEMA: Does it occur to you that there would be
some Hindu gangs also out there? Have to
be, I should think. Difficult to have a violent
confrontation with yourself; there *have*

to be two sides – both violent. Or do you think those Hindu gangs are out there only to protect us Hindus? Unfortunately we have two Muslims and a Christian with us in here. Maybe we should hide them. Lock them up in the store room with Mathew's cushions and curios or something.

VIKRAM: *(Ignoring the sarcasm in her tone.)*

They wouldn't be out there if it wasn't for these rioting Muslims. We have always been a peaceful people, accommodating by nature. That's what is wrong. We gave those Muslims too much leeway and now they want to grab our whole country, wipe us out.

(Reema laughs incredulously.
Rajesh, who has been sitting around numb, suddenly interrupts.)

RAJESH: Did she say Air Force? That Lady Minister? Are they going to bomb us?

(Looks at all the faces seeking an explanation.
Everybody just glances at him and then turns away ignoring him.)

SHANAZ: *(Also on edge)*

You think they are going to send out the whole Air Force just to bomb you? You? You think you are that important, you with your green and blue eye-shadows and blushers?

(Shanaz laughs harshly as if to relieve her own tension.
Rajesh colours)

RAJESH: I... I just thought s-s-she s-s-said...

(Looks ashamed and stops talking)

(Blackout for a moment.
Then only the footlights on the balcony come on to shine upwards on Rajesh standing on the balcony.
In the shadowy light on the rest of the stage, all others stay stock-still maintaining their positions.)

RAJESH: They all mock me and look down on me, even this bitch of a bar dancer. I *am* scared. I *am* frightened for my life. But then aren't they all? Even my big boss? Yet I am the one they all laugh at.
It has always been like this. Everybody has sneered at me, scorned me and turned away from me. I have been so lonely.
(Pause)
We have always been so poor, my father and my mother and my brothers and my sisters, all of us living in one room in a tenement. They all struggled to put me through the college and I couldn't get a job when I got my degree in hand. Most days I didn't dare to go home

because they all ranted at me for not getting a job. I was trying so hard but nobody would understand me or sympathise with me.

So after making those futile rounds of the offices I would just while the hours away in a teashop in the market sharing a cup of tea with anybody who was there. Purposeless, friendless, and broke. At last I got this stupid job of selling stupid things – something I can't stand, something I am no good at and something that pays a pittance. And it is also a lonely job: on road all the time, trying to charm strangers into buying things they don't want, getting doors banged in my face, eating lonely meals all by myself.

(Hangs his head in misery for a moment, then looks up again.)

There was this branch of one of those fanatical Hindu parties in front of the tea shop with pictures of many gods pasted all over it and I used to sit and watch its members strutting around, doing the puja together and singing bhajans together. There was such camaraderie amongst them. They moved together, they talked and laughed together, and they stood by each other. They had a purpose to their lives. I was so jealous of them.

I am not overly religious – sure I join my hands to the little idols on the shelf in the corner of the kitchen when my mother asks me to – but that's almost all. Yet, while passing, if one of those young men had said to me, 'come

Rajesh, come and join us,' wouldn't I have jumped up with alacrity? And wouldn't I have happily prayed to those gods with as great a fervour as them and sung all those bhajans with them? And I would have gladly worn one of those headbands that they all wear and shouted all those slogans while shaking my fist high up in the air like they do.

(Rajesh stands straight with one hand raised in a fist.)
I would have been one of them. I would have had friends to share my thoughts and my woes with; and also to laugh with, to enjoy life with. I wouldn't have been lonely anymore; I would have belonged.

(Pause)
And, now, at this time, in these riots, would I have marched with them?

(Sound of marching feet in the background.
Rajesh marches in place matching his steps to those sounds and with his one hand still raised in a fist.)
But would I have brandished a sword and a trident?

(Frenzied slogans being shouted are heard in the background.
Rajesh crouches down frightened, neck extended, looks tensely from side to side.
Speaks nervously in a low voice)
And would I have – would I have swung them at the women and children of the *Musalman* as they are feared to do?

(Background chanting : kill, kill.
Rajesh, looking deathly afraid, shrinks and pulls his head in like a turtle.

Pause
A man's voice recites in the background.
Rajesh stays stock-still.)

MAN'S VOICE: *(Reciting)*

Come little girls, come little boys,
it's time to play in the streets.
Bring your guns, bring your knives,
and chop each other into little bits.

(Pause)

RAJESH: No. No. Noooooo ... *I don't know...*
(Jumps up throwing his arms up and screaming.)
I Don't know!

(Blackout for a moment.
Then lights come on as before and all are in same
positions as before except for Rajesh who is sitting
on the chair holding his head in his hands.
Pause
Rajesh looks up.)

RAJESH: *(In an agonised voice)*

What would you do? What would any of you
do? What would anybody do?

CURTAIN

ACT IV

(Later the same night.

A single light focuses on the clock.

The clock shows and tolls 11.00 pm.

On the last toll of the clock all the lights come on flooding the stage with a strong bright light.

The walls of the lounge are bare. All the paintings except one small dull grey one on a side wall are gone. All the knickknacks and curios, all the cushions except one cushion which has fallen by the side of the sofa, the throw rugs and even the TV, the sideboard and some of the hard chairs have been taken away. Even the sofa cover has been removed to expose an old dull-grey undercover.

Only the ticking clock, the chandelier, the sofa and sofa chair, one hard chair, one small painting on the side wall and one cushion on the floor remain on the stage.

The stage is looking very empty, stark and desolate.

Shanaz is standing near the rear door hiding a large kitchen knife in her dupatta.

Vikram is sitting on the sofa staring straight ahead lost in his own thoughts.

Reema is sitting tight faced on the sofa chair watching Salim.

Salim, looking grim, his brow crinkled in deep thought, is standing by the window.

Jai is pacing the backstage.

Rajesh is sitting on the straight chair looking numb.

Mathew is not seen.

Shanaz finishes hiding the knife, ties the dupatta around her waist, goes through the rear door, comes out dragging a gas cylinder and moves towards the left archway, then stops, looks around, sees Rajesh and calls him.)

SHANAZ: Bring the other ones, Rajesh.

(Rajesh gets up and goes to her.)

RAJESH: What are you doing?

SHANAZ: *(Still bending over the cylinder)*

Bring those other gas cylinders. We will line them up by the front door.

(Rajesh looks confused.)

RAJESH: What for?

(Shanaz straightens up and looks him in the face.)

SHANAZ: *(Aggressively)*

They won't take me alive this time. They come for me, they go with me.

(Rajesh flinches and backs away from her.)

SHANAZ: *(Looks at Rajesh with contempt.)*

All right then, don't help me. I can manage by myself; I have always managed by myself. You go and sit in a corner like a good little boy.

(Rajesh, who is sitting down again, looks at her with loathing.
Mathew enters from the right archway looking dishevelled.)

MATHEW: *(Rubbing his hands together)*

Well, that is the lot I think – oh, there is still one painting hanging there. Anything else?

(Looks around and sees Shanaz dragging the cylinder, stands in shock for a moment watching her and then rushes to her and wrenches the cylinder out of her hands.)

MATHEW: What are you up to, woman? You want to burn down this resort? You are mad. Get away from there, get away.

(Shanaz stands arms akimbo watching him wheel the cylinder back towards the rear door.)

SHANAZ: It's quite clear to anybody what I am up to, you moron.

(Mathew stops and looks at her startled. Then takes the cylinder out through the rear door.
Shanaz turns her nose up at him and turns away.
Lights on the stage dim.
Only one light focuses on Shanaz's face.

Everybody stays still.
Shanaz's voice-over is heard in background.)

SHANAZ'S
VOICE-OVER:

They won't take me alive this time, not like the last time. And this time when I go I will take at least some of them with me. The first one who comes near me gets a knife in his stomach. And the rest will go up in smoke even if I go with them.

I remember that last riot – how can I ever forget it? How frightened and helpless I had felt. And then, the flight; flight to where? They were everywhere.

Never free. Never free to do, to be, what I like. Always in fear of men, always at some man's mercy. That's what I have been.

(Pause
A man's voice is heard reciting in the background.
Shanaz stands still, glowering at the space in front.)

MAN'S VOICE: *(Reciting)*

When the itinerant to my city talks
of his midnight walks
through its deserted roads to the seaside rocks
to watch the moon shine,
or of his lonely climb to its wooded hilltop
to sit and wait for the dawn to rise,
a great fury rises in my heart.

For though this has always been my city
these simple pleasures for me are not to be

simply because
I was born to wear a sari.

(Pause)

SHANAZ'S
VOICE-OVER: But I am not that same frightened, cowardly, Shanaz anymore. Now I am someone who is not afraid to fight back; someone who is not afraid to die. I have been afraid of them for so long. Not anymore. Not now.

(Lights come on as before.)

SHANAZ: *(Loudly)*

Now *I* will make them fear *me*.

(Rajesh stares at her wild eyed.
Shanaz sees Rajesh staring at her and grins disparagingly at him.)

SHANAZ: *(To Rajesh)*

I don't need to worry about you, little boy. You are already afraid of everything.

(Rajesh looks away quivering with rage.
Lights on the stage dim.
Only one light focuses on Rajesh's face.
Everybody stays still.
Rajesh's voice-over is heard in the background.)

RAJESH'S
VOICE-OVER:

How dare she talk to me like that? What is she after all – a street walker by any name. And while I may not have the money she makes, still I am from a respectable family, doing a respectable job. She is dirt but even she treats me like a... like a –

(Suddenly breaks down and starts sobbing.
Voice-over continues.)

Even *she* knows that nobody accepts me, nobody pays any attention to me, nobody cares for me; they all ignore me. She knows that I am all alone and I am nothing on my own.

(Rajesh raises his head looking devastated but also determined.)

I have to join up with them – they are out there now. Then I will belong with somebody, I will be part of a group. Then nobody will dare to order me around like a serf or treat me with contempt. Nobody will dare that because they – they with their headbands showing that they are a group – they all will be with me, they all will stand by me. I will not be alone anymore. I *have to* join up with them.

(Lights come on as before.)

RAJESH:

(Wiping his cheeks, sitting up straight, loudly)

I *have* to join up with them. I *will* be part of their group. I will belong. At last I will belong. And they will always be there for me –

(Everybody is staring at him in incomprehension. Jai goes up to him and grasps his arm, interrupting him.)

JAI: What the heck are you talking about, kid?

(A burst of gunfire is heard in the distance. Everybody, startled, turns to the window and listens wide-eyed, alarmed by the sounds outside. Mathew comes running back through the rear door and stops watching.)

RAJESH: *(To Jai, in a rushing manner)*

They are also out there. The *Musalman*s are also out there. They are coming to kill us. Can't you hear them? I am going.

(Shakes off Jai's hand and jumps up. Jai moves back but watches him with concern.)

JAI: Going where, kid? Didn't you just say the *Musalman*s are out there?

RAJESH: *(Ignoring Jai, to all of them, wildly)*

There is another gang there also; there are two of them, coming up and down the road; that's what that secretary said. The other one will be of Hindus. I am going to join them.

SALIM: *(Grimly waving him down)*

Sit down kid. In here you have at least a modicum of a chance to escape them, to survive; out there you will have none. They may both be Muslim gangs for all we know. And even if one of them or even both of them are of Hindus, they are not going to stop and ask you your religion and caste before they chop you up. Not in the frenzied state that they are in. They are just bursting to chop up and burn everybody and everything in their way. I know. I have been through it. So you just sit exactly where you are.

RAJESH: *(Babbling)*

One of those gangs will be of Hindus. It will. It will. And they will know me. They will accept me. I will be one of them. Then I will have a cause. I am going to join them. I am going.

(Shouting)

I AM GOING. I AM GOING.

*(Runs out through the left archway.
Others watch him go in stunned silence.
Vikram has been leaning forward, has also been
watching Rajesh with concern.)*

VIKRAM: *(Softly, to himself)*

God help that poor kid.

(Reema looks at him surprised.)

REEMA: You care for the fate of your lowly worker? I would have thought you cared only for your own fate.

VIKRAM: *(Still looking through the archway.)*

He is courting death; we are awaiting death. Not much difference in the ultimate outcome.
(Looks at Reema and sits back)
The tiny bit of difference, Namrata, is that he has latched on to a plausible chance and shown some courage in going headlong to meet his fate while we prefer to stay here hanging by a very slender thread of hope.
It is that hope that keeps us still sitting here, waiting for providence to solve all our problems. And like all those who live on hope, we also shall be losers.

REEMA: *(Trying to sound sarcastic and failing)*

What do you propose we should do, Vikram? Run out like him? Where to?

VIKRAM: We are in a fix, Namrata, there is no doubt about that. There is nowhere for us to run to. If they come this far, they will overrun this whole area far faster than we can run. That kid, he made a decision – right or wrong – and acted on it. You have to admire an act like that; especially in the face of possibility of certain death.

(Reema looks thoughtfully at him as at a stranger and then sits back watching him.
Jai is still standing where he was, still looking through the left archway.)

JAI: *(To himself)*

That kid is very keen to die.

SALIM: *(Also looking through the archway)*

Everybody needs a cause to die for.

JAI: Perhaps. And perhaps some people need a cause to live for.

(Salim turns and gives him a long speculative look and then moves back to the window.
Jai goes and joins Salim at the window.)

JAI: *(Shaking his head in frustration.)*

This stupid, meaningless, purposeless violence! What do they expect to gain by this wanton killing of defenceless people – women and children? If you have a cause that you believe in, then fight those who oppose you, those who stand in your way barring you. Fight for a purpose; don't go on a mindless rampage.

(Reflectively)

I have always known I will die of a bullet. I chose my cause. I live by bullet, I will die by bullet. But with both my feet braced against the earth and with a gun in my hand. Never thought I would go like this.

SALIM: I am not afraid of death; I lost that fear in the last riot.
When I started on my path I too expected to die of a gun; and also in a gunfight, a face-to-face fight. Fight like a man, die like a man. Not like this – cornered like a rat in a useless killing spree.

(Pause
A man's voice recites in the background.
Jai and Salim stay stock-still.)

MAN'S VOICE: *(Reciting)*

He will die unsung some day
on some obscure battlefield
fighting for a lost cause
that mattered to none other than he.

(Pause)

SALIM: I too chose my cause long ago. And I started weighing everything in the balance of practicality blindfolded like the statue of justice to any other aspect of it. I piled my emotions behind what I thought was an unbreakable dam.

(Salim turns to face away from Jai.
Lights on the stage dim.
A single light focuses on Salim's face.
Jai stays still.
Salim's voice-over is heard in the background.)

SALIM'S
VOICE-OVER: One strange quirk of fate, one chance meeting –
Now the only song I know is the one that had died in me a long time ago.
And it questions my path.
Once there was another path, the one that my Sufi mentor showed me – Once? Was?

(Pause
All the stage lights come on.
Salim is looking very unsure of himself.
Pause
Firing and blasts are heard again in the distance.
For a moment all are mesmerised by the sound and stare out of the window.
Then Shanaz goes and sits on the chair vacated by Rajesh.
Mathew mechanically takes the last painting off the wall and goes through the right archway.
Vikram is still sitting traumatised by Rajesh's exit.
Reema is still watching Vikram.
Jai looks everybody over and then turns to Salim.)

JAI: There comes a time, Salim, when you have to

weigh your priorities and make a choice and the choice isn't easy. But you have no option.

*(Salim looks at him questioningly but does not speak.
Lights on the stage dim.
A single light focuses on Jai and Salim.)*

JAI: *(In a low voice.)*

There is a way out of here, isn't there?

(Salim looks at him for a long moment.)

SALIM: So you *have* made up your mind as to the path you will take.

JAI: Tribals badly need any help they can get, Salim.
(Pause)
There is a way out, isn't there?
(Salim doesn't answer; just keeps looking at him.)
Stands to reason. I didn't have any time to case the joint or even get any info about this area; but *you* wouldn't hole up in a place without scouting it first and making sure there is an alternate way out if they ever came for you. Especially after your last experience.
(Smiles a grim smile)
Jungle logic.

*(Salim nods but doesn't speak.
Jai keeps looking at him.
Pause
Jai waits.)*

SALIM: It's tough, Jai, a bit too tough. It's not for everyone. You won't be able to make it.

JAI: I will risk it.

SALIM: *(Shaking his head)*

             Same old Jai. You will risk anything to get back to your people. Nothing else has ever mattered to you but your cause.

JAI: What else is there in life, Salim?

             (Salim doesn't reply.)

JAI: It's the river, isn't it?

SALIM: You can't swim.

JAI: I learnt it in the jungle. You have to learn a lot of things in the jungle if you want to survive.

SALIM: It's not just a simple swim across the river. There is no safety on the other side either.

JAI: Survival in a jungle also needs a lot of different techniques of swimming.

             (Salim stays quiet.
             Jai waits looking at him.
             After a while Salim looks him over and then nods again.)

SALIM: If you sneak past the village temple and go down the lane, there is a dip in the ground that will let you slip unnoticed into the river. Swim upriver – don't go downriver, mind you, though the current is very strong and will keep pushing you downriver but there are crocodile pools down there and those crocs tear up into tiny bits any living body that comes within their reach, indiscriminately and mindlessly.

JAI: *(Smiling grimly)*

Even Naxalites?

SALIM: *(Smiles in return.)*

Even Naxalites. And even Muslim terrorists. Along with the meek and the innocents. They neither discriminate nor do they wait until they are hungry. And they find neither any joy in it nor have any qualms about it. They see you, they attack you. It's their country down there. Anyway, keep to the right bank and you will have to swim underwater most of the time because they are sure to have a couple of watchers up on the bridge. After a few miles you will come to a small creek that leads to a swamp with mangroves and strands of reeds. Grab a reed, they are hollow already you know, put one end in your mouth to breathe through, make sure the other end is over the waterline, hold on to the mangrove roots and settle down in the mud to wait them out.

Nobody will ever come looking for you over there though they may do a surface check of the river and the swamp.

JAI: *(Thoughtfully)*

I could do that.

SALIM: *(In a warning tone)*

It may be a long wait. Army or police may come in after the rioters and for you they are equally if not more dangerous than these rioters. In time you can wade in the creek and get to the coast. Fishermen there ask no questions about a passage to anywhere if the money is right.

JAI: *(Watching him)*

I assume you are not coming.

SALIM: You know, my friend, that I have to stay here.

*(Pause
Jai glances back at Reema.)*

JAI: She let you down. She chose her father over you.

SALIM: It's not about what *she* did or didn't do. It's about what *I* can and can't do.

JAI: You weighed everything in the balance of practicality, you said. It's a fight for justice, you said. Doesn't it matter anymore?

(Salim doesn't reply.)

JAI: *(Sighs)*

I always believed in letting a man choose his own destiny but in your case I will break my own rule.
(Looks earnestly at Salim.)
Martyrs never accomplish anything, Salim. Alive, you can keep up the fight. Dead, you are dead. Lenin said that.

SALIM: Do you see me leaving her alone to face this terror?

JAI: One night. One night. That's all that was needed to change you, to change all your priorities.

(More bursts of gunfire are heard in the distance.)

SALIM: You had better leave. They are getting closer every moment.

JAI: This crazy, stupid love.

*(Looks at Salim and then puts a hand on Salim's shoulder and squeezes it.
Salim puts his hand on his arm.)*

SALIM: Good luck.

                  (Jai slips out of the back door.
                  Nobody notices.
                  Lights come on as before.
                  Salim turns to the window.
                  Pause
                  Mathew comes rushing in from the
                  right archway.)

MATHEW: That takes care of all the paintings. Now
                  everything that could be looted is locked up
                  in the store room.

                  (Looks up)

                  The chandelier. I must hide that chandelier.

                  (Looks around frantically for something to climb
                  upon and doesn't find anything suitable.)

                  Mr Joseph, Mr Joseph, could you get that
                  chandelier down for me?

                  (Salim keeps looking out of the window.)

MATHEW: *(Loudly)*

                  Mr Joseph.

SALIM: *(Still looking out of the window.)*

                  There is a river out there.

MATHEW: What?

SALIM: Rivers flow. Rivers lead to somewhere. Rivers are lifelines.

MATHEW: *(Loudly)*

            Mr Joseph, can you get this chandelier down for me?

            (Salim turns, looks at Mathew and starts laughing at him.
            Mathew stares at him for a moment then shakes his head and rushes back through the right archway.
            Shanaz is still sitting looking down, lost in her thoughts.
            Reema, startled, looks at Salim for a moment and then turns back to watch Vikram.
            Vikram is sitting rigid on the sofa with his fingertips pressed into his temples staring into nothing.)

VIKRAM: *(To himself)*

            This is not the time to die.

            (Lights on the stage dim.
            Only one light focuses on Vikram.
            Vikram's voice-over is heard in the background.)

VIKRAM'S
VOICE-OVER: I am still on my way, almost there, to where I have always hankered to be and then this has to happen. Just a little more time and

my company also would have been an A-1 company. Why should this happen to me now? I have so much more to achieve yet.

This is not the time to die. Death should come at a dignified old age after your sons have taken over what you have built and you have watched them build on the top of it – watched them and guided them. It should come after you have spent your retirement age joyfully playing with your grandsons. It should come to you peacefully while you are surrounded by your family. Not like this, not like this. Not until you have achieved and settled everything that you set out to do. Not while everything is still in a limbo.

(Light moves to include Reema.)

(Loudly)

No, this is not the time to die.

(Vikram looks up to find Reema watching him. Moves his hands down, sits back and looks pensively at her.)

I never mistreated you, Namrata. I was never nasty to you or abused you or was physically violent to you.

REEMA: *(Gravely)*

No.

VIKRAM: In the beginning, after our marriage, actually I was quite in awe of you. I was ready to do anything for you, to be your slave. But you didn't want me. In a way I understood that; I wasn't of your class yet. Then, when I had found my feet in the factory and in the business, when I had gained my confidence to deal successfully with life, when I had proved myself, I had thought I would come to you and say, 'Look Namrata, I have brought the moon down for you' and you would recognise something of value in me, would return my love. But even then you made it clear that you didn't care for me. And I accepted even that. I left you to your own pursuits, never commented on them and concentrated on expanding the business. I even ignored all the gossip, rumours and gibes that came my way and made my own place in the society in spite of them.

(Reema nods watching him. Her face is softening and a hint of pity has appeared in her eyes.)

I only asked you to give me a son, Namrata. Who do I leave all this to – all this that I have strived so hard to build – when I am gone?

(Reema's eyes are full of pity.)

And now it seems I will be gone much sooner than I expected. Why, Namrata, why? This is not the time to die. Why do I have to die at this time? Tell me why.

(Reema goes to him and kneels by him.)

REEMA: *(Softly and tenderly)*

There is no reason to it, Vikram. There is no rhyme or rhythm to this violence. It just is.

(Vikram keeps looking at her.
Reema looks at him compassionately)

REEMA: But it is still possible, Vikram, that they will bypass this resort. They aren't interested in Christians or their resorts. Also it *is* far in from the highway. You heard Jai. We all could very well come out of this without a scratch.

(Vikram looks at her neutrally.)

VIKRAM: You think so, Namrata?

(Reema puts a reassuring hand on his hand.)

REEMA: We will, Vikram, believe me, we all will come out of this unharmed. You just stay here for a few days and when everything quietens, you can go back home, safe and sound.

(Vikram smiles disbelievingly.)

REEMA: *(Looking into his eyes)*

You *will* go home safely, Vikram, believe me, you will.

VIKRAM: *I* will, Namrata?

(Pause
Reema involuntarily glances at Salim.
Vikram notices and also looks at Salim. His lips tighten.

Reema looks down for a moment, and then resolutely continues back to Vikram.)

REEMA: And when all this is over, I will talk to Shanaz, Vikram. I will appease her, make her understand what this baby means to you. You can find her a good nursing home in the hills to stay in and then, later, you can adopt the baby. Nobody needs to know. It's your baby, Vikram, it should be brought up in your house.

(Vikram throws her hand off his and cringes back from her while glowering at her at the same time.)

VIKRAM: A baby with a *Muslim* woman as his mother? *I* should bring up a *Muslim* woman's baby in *my* house? Treat him as *my* heir? Nobody needs to know, hah! He will still have that Muslim blood running through his veins. You are out of your mind!

(Reema looks as if she has been slapped and falls back on her haunches.
Lights brighten on the stage.
Reema wordlessly gets up and moves away turning her back on Vikram, stands still for a long moment and then rushes to Salim.)

REEMA: *(Grabbing Salim's arms and shaking him.)*

What is going on here, Salim? Why this sudden callousness, sudden aggression from everybody? Why this sudden killing spree out there? *You* are a killer. *You* tell me.

SALIM: *(Disengaging his arms and holding her gently)*

Yes, I am a killer. Yes, I kill. But then we all would like to kill; one way or another: physically, or verbally; or emotionally or socially. Violence is not only a physical outburst, Reema, it comes in many hues. Words kill in a far cruel manner. Words burrow inside your mind and kill you slowly, a little every day. As does scorn. And overwhelming love also can smother you. We are all potential killers, Reema.

REEMA: *(Still aggressively)*

You turned a killer to control killing. *You* turned a terrorist to control terrorism. *You,* you stood right there and lectured me a while ago about chopping off the head to make the body wither and die. So why aren't you controlling this madness now? Why are you just standing there singing to yourself? You want help? Do you? I am here.

SALIM: *(Shaking his head)*

It is too late now Reema; and who knows if there ever was a head to it or if there were many small heads – most of them insignificant – that have led it to this.

Nobody knows where and how it started or how it spread all over the country. Any small excuse or rumour or even an insignificant incidence – incited or something that just happened and was used by somebody for his profit – could have brought this about. But now it has become self-propelled. It is mass hysteria now, Reema. And when it generates a momentum of its own, then the leaders lie low and let the people face the brunt of it.

Now there is nothing we can do to stop it, Reema.

(With a wry smile)

Now we are the people, Reema, we are the people who don't subscribe to this mindless violence but, unfortunately, that also makes us the weak and helpless ones who have no recourse against it. Now we just have to wait – for it to either engulf us or to pass us by. That's all we can do.

(Reema stares at him for a long moment and then despondently rests her head on his arm.
Vikram suddenly jumps up brandishing a gun.)

VIKRAM: *(Pointing the gun at Salim)*

Get away from her, get away from my wife, you, you *Musalman*.

(Reema lifts her head.
Salim tenses.)

SALIM: That's my gun. No wonder I couldn't find it. I thought may be Jai... but he would never do that. How did you get it?

VIKRAM: *(Waving the gun about)*

You are a Muslim terrorist and you are here amongst us during these riots. You think I – I who have had to deal with the factory labour risings all the time – wouldn't search your cottage? Hah! You will be the first one I kill, you *Musalman*! And then I will kill them all, each and everybody. I have the power here, understand?

(Reema moves before Salim and spreads her arms around him.
Shanaz stands up suddenly attracting Vikram's attention.
Vikram looks at her with disdain.)

VIKRAM: *(Spits the words out at her)*

Bitch! Whore!

(Shanaz draws her shoulders back and looks him in the eye.)

SHANAZ: And you, you who took advantage of my need for your money to force a child on me without my consent, what does it make you?

(Vikram turns on her almost incensed.

Mathew comes through the right archway, stops on seeing Vikram with the gun and then tries to creep away along the sofa.
Vikram notices him, swings around and turns his gun on him.
Mathew, mouth agape, falls back on the sofa.)

MATHEW: I... I...I have n...n...not s...s...said any–

VIKRAM: You! You will be next, you Christian! You Christians are all the same. You have been trying to convert us to Christianity all this time, haven't you?

MATHEW: *(Eyes rolling)*

Me?

(Salim has pushed Reema back and is quietly moving towards Vikram.
Vikram swivels and points the gun at Salim.
Salim stops dead.
Sounds of blasts and firing are heard outside and intermittent red flashes show in the windows.
Vikram turns to the window.
All stare out of the window transfixed for a moment and then turn to look at Vikram again as he starts shouting.)

VIKRAM: *(Waving his gun at the window.)*

So they have come, have they? They think they can get me, *me:* Vikram Dixit, CEO of

a vast industry, Managing Director of tea estates and a leading figure in business?
(Shouting)
I will show those bastards who gets who. *I* will teach them a lesson for taking me on. *I* will show them what it means to oppose me, to threaten me. *I* will show them who is in charge here, who has the power here...
(Runs out through the left archway still shouting and waving his gun high.)
I will show you who has the power here, you bastards, *I* will show you...

REEMA: *(Running after him and calling)*

Vikram, Vikram...

(Vikram's shouts can be heard diminishing in loudness until they fade.
Everybody has stayed frozen staring at the archway through which Vikram has gone.
Sounds of blasts and firing have subsided but red flashes in the windows are still seen once in a while.
Reema is standing still, rooted in the archway.
Long pause
Salim moves up to Reema and holds her arm.)

REEMA: *(Looking straight ahead through the archway into nothingness, in an impersonal, toneless voice)*

He was never like this. He was not an egoist though he has always been ambitious. Money, prestige, power, especially power was what drove him. He was ruthless in business, he ran the factories with an iron hand and he personified power in the world of commerce. But he was never violent.

(Looks up at Salim)

He was never prejudiced religiously either; his brother is; but he dealt impartially with Hindus and Muslims all the time; not only in the factories and in business but he mixed with the Muslims socially also. We had them coming to the house for dinner and went to their houses all the time.

(Pause

Reema turns to look through the archway again.)

Last month, just before Bakri-id, we were driving through Bhiwandi and a goat ran out on the road. Vikram swerved to avoid it and the car landed in a deep pothole. A group of Muslim men were standing around chitchatting but when they saw the running goat and lopsided car, they left the goat alone and instead came running over to the car and picked it up out of the pothole, all of them laughing and happy and the children who were running after the goat came over and were jumping around and Vikram smiled and joked with them and thanked them and gave money to the children to buy sweets.

(Looks up at Salim again)

Some of them could be part of that gang out there baying for our blood right now, couldn't they? And some of them could fall victim to Vikram's bullets.

(Salim gently guides her away from the archway and to the window.
Lights dim on the stage.
Only one light focuses on Reema and Salim.)

REEMA: *(Looking far away into the distance, in a low voice.)*

I nettled him. I nettled him in every way I could. I nettled him all these years to an unbearable extent. I snubbed him, I taunted him and I belittled him all the time because I wanted him to pay the price for being a fortune hunter, for marrying me for Daddy's wealth and especially for taking me away from you. I kept goading him on because I wanted him to break. But he never rose to the bait; he was always polite to me, almost deferential. He kept his dignity.
(Turns and looks at the sofa where Vikram had been sitting, her eyes anguished, her face remorseful.)
And when he did break, all I felt was pity. And abysmal disgust.

SALIM: Pity *and* disgust for him?

REEMA: Pity for him. Disgust at myself.

(Reema turns and rests her head on the window jamb. Her shoulders sag.
Both stay quiet for a long moment.
Then Salim speaks over her head.)

SALIM: All I have ever wanted was you in my arms

and a song on my lips. When I heard of your marriage, the person I was most angry with was you. Yet I also wanted to protect you and I also wanted to hit out – at somebody, anybody.
I wanted to kill.
My Sufi mentor showed me the other side, made me aware of the other way, and I was totally taken up with that other way of love and brotherhood. But the wound in the heart was still there and the anger had only gone dormant; it was not extinguished. And I was even then all ready to hit out at anybody who challenged that side of Islam that I had come to love.
Those last riots were only a catalyst, a spark that rekindled that fire to kill within me.

REEMA: *(Pulls her head back and looks bewildered at Salim.)*

You were the farthest from a killer that I could have ever imagined, Salim. What is happening to us all? We are supposed to be educated, sensible, peaceful people.
(Looking away, to herself)
Where does this sudden urge surface in all of us, the urge to hurt, to kill? Why do we suddenly change our nature? What's behind this complete breakdown of all our moral concepts, this total submission to this violence not intrinsic to us?

SALIM: *(Answering her monologue)*

The same reason that makes a mother raise

her hand to a child she loves or makes a gentle, quiet man fly into a road-rage or even makes a studious schoolboy pick up a gun and shoot his schoolmates. Violence *is* intrinsic to us, Reema.

What your father did to you, was it not violence? When you decided on revenge because you had been cheated, because a gross injustice had been done to you, what was it? Was it not violence against your father and Vikram? When you went on a promiscuous spree that you hated, was it not violence against your own self?

(Reema looks at him startled.)

Because there is an instinct for violence in the back of our psyche in all of us, Reema. An instinct controlled by our life instincts like our desire for love and pleasure, by our need for relationships and by our conscience.

And when that control is lost, whether from birth or by circumstance, for whatever the reason or no reason at all, justifiably or otherwise, then the instinct for violence surfaces and the casualty is love, honour and morals. When there is nothing left to lose, the masks fall off and our primal instincts come forth. Then we just want to hurt, in any way we can, sometimes others and sometimes even our own selves.

And then, when it becomes a totally mindless violence which over-rides everything and when nothing else matters to you, then,

Reema, you are in crocodile country. Then you have to take a stock of yourself if you want to exit it again.

REEMA: There is no time left to take stock of oneself, is there Salim?
          (Looking out of the window and shivering)
          This is the end.

SALIM: *(Gently)*

          I am afraid so, Reema.

          (Lights brighten on the stage.
          Blasts and firing are heard again, closer this time.
          Red flashes show in the windows.)

MATHEW: *(Suddenly jumping up and rushing around)*

          They are coming. They are coming here, *here*. Run, run.

SALIM: *(Turning to him)*

          Run where, Mathew?

MATHEW: Out! Out! To the village! Everything valuable is locked up in the store room. It will be safe. We can run. We can hide in the village.

          (Salim laughs. A short laugh.)

SALIM: You think they will spare the village after

coming so far inside from the highway? They will burn the village, both halves of it, Hindu and Muslim. The Hindu gang will burn the Muslim half and the Muslim one will burn the Hindu half. Then one or the other of them will torch this resort.

They are not out to loot, Mathew, they are out to kill, to burn, to destroy; looting is only incidental. This is annihilation, Mathew. They will burn all and everything that they come across and in the end all that will be left will be ashes. Where do you want to run to? Neither the village nor the riverside offer any refuge. The river banks are devoid of any trees and you can see miles and miles of them from the bridge. Wouldn't we have run long before this if there was a place to run to?

There is no place left to run to, Mathew, nowhere to hide, and no way to avoid this carnage.

This is the end.

(Mathew stops in his rush, stares at Salim for a long moment with his mouth open and then goes and subsides back on the sofa in a daze.)

MATHEW: *(To himself.)*

Burn? Burn? Burn all this? This is the end?
(Looks around the room)
They will burn all this? They will burn all my furniture, my pantry with the stock of food, my chandelier, my store room with everything

I so painstakingly collected? They will burn my resort? All the rooms and cottages?

(Collapses on the sofa covering his face.
Lights on the stage dim.
Only one light focuses on Mathew's face.
Everybody stays still.
Mathew's voice-over is heard in the background.)

MATHEW'S
VOICE-OVER: They will burn everything. They will reduce to ashes what I mortgaged my soul for.
(Sobbing)
I will lose everything, everything I have. They will burn everything.
(Pause
Sitting up)
No. No. The Almighty will not let them do it. He will stop them. He will... And yet – and yet -
(His shoulders sag again)
And yet the Home Minister had lied to us. Deviji does not care for us. The police also will not protect us though she had promised us that they will. What if The Almighty also won't protect us? What if He also has forsaken us? No, no, no...
(Pause
Mathew starts sobbing again.
Pause
Mathew suddenly looks up, wipes his tears, sits up straight and squares his shoulders.
Mathew's voice-over continues.)
If everybody has forsaken me, if they all have left my resort to the thuggery of these rioters,

then... then... then I will have to protect my resort on my own. I will have to defend it by myself. I will have to defend it by any means that are available to me.

(Lights brighten on the stage.
Mathew looks around, sees Shanaz sitting on the chair and rushes to her.)

MATHEW: You want help with those gas cylinders, Shanaz? I will help you.

(Man's voice speaks authoritatively in the background)

MAN'S VOICE: Thou shalt not kill.

(Mathew, startled, looks upwards.)

MATHEW: *(Looking upwards)*

I have always been a good Christian. All my life I have tried to live by the Ten Commandments. And now, when all that I have struggled to achieve is in danger, is there any help from the Almighty? Why, for what sin of mine, has He forsaken me: me, an innocent; me, His faithful?
Now I will deal with this as *I* see fit.

(Man's voice again speaks authoritatively in the background)

MAN'S VOICE: Whosoever shall kill shall be in danger of
                 the judgement.

MATHEW: *(Shouts to the sky)*

                 Even Deuteronomy has said that if the
                 circumstances warrant it, then 'thou shall
                 smite every man'.
                 If you won't help me, then leave me alone;
                 leave me alone to do what I think is right
                 even if it is not right by you.
                 (Turns to Shanaz)
                 Come, Shanaz.

                 *(Grabs Shanaz's arm and tries to pull her to
                 the kitchen.*
                 Shanaz disengages her arm and sits down again.)

SHANAZ: *(Pointing at the red flashes outside the
                 window, gloomily)*

                 Doesn't matter anymore. Can't you hear
                 those blasts and see those flames? They
                 will have missiles of their own to throw,
                 like grenades and flaming torches, that they
                 can throw from a distance and still keep
                 themselves safe.

                 (Mathew looks at the window.)

MATHEW: *(Looking around frantically)*

                 So what can we throw at them?

SHANAZ: *(Sarcastically)*

What will you throw, Mathew? Curios? Flaming cushions?
(Sags down again)
There is nothing to throw and nowhere left to run to, Mathew.
This is the end.

((Lights on the stage dim.
Only one light focuses on Shanaz.
Mathew maintains his position.
Shanaz's voice-over is heard in the background.)

SHANAZ'S
VOICE-OVER: This is the end. They have played games with me all my life and now they have won. I am utterly helpless again.
(Pause)
Maybe. Maybe this *is* the end, but then again, maybe it is not. I have lived through so much, I may live even through this. Then what? Make them fear me? How?
(Pause)
I will find a way. I will have to.
(Lifts her head and straightens her shoulders.)
But my only asset is my body. I can use my body to attract them and then I can destroy them.
(Looks at Salim's back.)
Or there is Salim's way.
(Pause)
I will choose if I get the chance to.

(Lights brighten on the stage.

*Shanaz lifts her head and squares her shoulders
and looks at Mathew almost viciously.)*

SHANAZ: That's what I will do, Mathew.

*(Mathew stares at her in shock for a moment. Then
his shoulders sag and he collapses back on the sofa.)*

MATHEW: *(Looks around dazed. Mutters to himself)*

Nothing to do. No way to fight them. Nothing
to throw at them. No way to defend my
resort. No place to run to. No place to hide.
Just wait. Wait. Wait for them to come and
end it all. That's all.
This is the end.

*(Long pause
Mathew is sitting crumpled on the sofa.
Shanaz is sitting tight-lipped on the straight chair
looking straight ahead.
Reema and Salim are standing at the window
looking out.
There is an air about them all of waiting for
the inevitable.
Gunfire is heard outside. Red flashes show in
the windows.
Mathew, still in a daze, looks at the window,
then around the room as if taking a last look at
everything, sees the cushion lying on the floor,
stares at it for a long moment as if confused by
it, then gets up, picks it up without thinking and
shuffles out through the archway at right.*

Mathew's scream is heard through the right archway.
All eyes turn towards the right archway.
Mathew, terrified, runs on to the stage.)

MATHEW:

(Stopping in the middle of the stage and turning around to look through the right archway, in an agitated state)

There is someone back there.

(Shanaz jumps up.
Salim pushes Reema back and quickly moves towards the right archway groping in his waist-band.
Reema puts a hand on his arm and stays him.)

REEMA:

You don't have a gun anymore.

(Salim stops and then flattens himself against the wall by the archway all coiled up to spring.
They all wait looking apprehensively at the archway.
Pause
A black-robed stooping old Christian priest holding a rosary in his hand slowly shambles in through the archway.
They watch him dumbfounded.)

PRIEST:

I was just seeking a shelter. They burned my church. They burned the Lord's house. It was not even on the highway. It was in a meadow behind the village. It was empty at this time with nobody left to defend it, all the faithful having already run away like deserters. I was in the barn at the back when I saw it burst

174

into flames. I have been wandering around since then when somebody told me that there is a Christian resort here. I thought I might find someone here who needs God's help, who needs a prayer, a hand to hold.

(Looks around at everybody and sees Salim. Takes a step back, shocked.)

You! You are still alive. All those wounds, all that blood... yet you have recovered. Praise be to our all merciful Lord.

SALIM: *(Coldly)*

No thanks to you though.

(The priest keeps staring at Salim while slowly backing to the sofa, sits down heavily and hangs his head. His hands holding the Rosary are trembling. Salim gives him a long cold look and then turns his back on him and goes to stand looking out of the window.
Shanaz sits down on the hard chair again staring at the priest.
Mathew is standing by the wall looking stunned.
Reema looks at the priest and then at Salim's back and then again at the priest and then goes and sits down on the sofa next to the priest.)

REEMA: *(To the priest)*

He came to you for help once, didn't he?

(The priest doesn't speak or look up.)

REEMA: *(Repeats aggressively)*

Didn't he, Father?

PRIEST: *(In a low tremulous voice, still looking down)*

It was during the last riots.

REEMA: He came all wounded and bloodied to the door of your God's house seeking succour but you looked at him horrified and said, 'You are not a Christian'.

PRIEST: *(Still in a low voice)*

I am so ashamed of my behaviour of that night. I have repented it many times since then. I have prayed many times for his recovery, for his well-being. God will forgive me.

REEMA: *(Bitterly)*

You didn't help him when he sorely needed your help. You banged the door of your God's house on his face. And you call yourself a Christian, a God's man! Where was your Christian compassion, love and charity then? And now you pray and say your God will forgive you!

PRIEST: *(Looks up straight at Reema)*

We all make mistakes that we regret, child. We all do something that later on we wish we hadn't done and we all don't do something that later on we wish we had. God understands our human fallibilities. He is all merciful.

REEMA: That was not a mistake. That was prejudice; pure and simple, unmitigated prejudice. You could have then shown to him this all-encompassing mercy of your God that you talk about now. You could have healed him, talked to him, shown him the right way by setting an example. Instead, by your action, you confirmed him on the path that he chose that night.

PRIEST: There are many things done during violent times, child, evil things, heartless things. Perhaps out of prejudice, perhaps out of fear or perhaps also because of selfish interests.

I have thought many times about my reason for my action of that night. Was it prejudice? Or was it cowardice? Or was it a justifiable fear, fear of not knowing who he was – perhaps a terrorist himself come there with intents of violence? Fear for the safety of the faithful who had taken shelter in there? Or fear of not knowing who else was following him, who else would barge into God's house to desecrate it?

It is the fear of the unknown, child, that makes it hard for any of us to make a proper choice, to behave humanely.

REEMA:
Perhaps it was just self-interest – fear for your own personal safety.

PRIEST:
(Emphatically)

No, child. The fear for my own life has never deterred me from any action. When we enter the Lord's service, we put our lives into His hands to do with them as He pleases. The thought of my own safety would never override my faith in Him in any situation.
(Pause
Looks meditatively at Reema.)
And you, child, did he come to you then? Did you help him? Did he tell you what path he had chosen, what he was going to do with his life in future? And did you try to deter him from it?

(Reema, startled, stares at him wordlessly.
Pause
· *Lights dim on stage.*
Only one light focuses on Reema.
Reema's voice-over is heard in the background.)

REEMA'S
VOICE-OVER:
That was what I dreamed about, much later; much, much later. In that dream that was what they all kept asking me, shouting at me while encircling me, hedging me in. 'He came to you that night, you met him that night,' they accused me. Over and over, again and again, they said, 'He told you, he told you that night,' and I screamed 'No. No. No.'

Yet he had come to me that night, I did meet him that one night. After I had given up on my search of him, he had come knocking on my door. 'I have come to say goodbye, Reema,' he had said. 'Let's run away,' I had said to him. 'Let's run away from this world into a different world, Salim,' I had said, 'a world of love and music and singing.' But he only shook his head. 'It's too late, Reema. I have come to say goodbye.' he had said.

Was it just a dream or did it really happen? Was it true or did I imagine it? I don't know, I don't know till to-date but I understood it when I saw that murky, grainy photograph in the newspapers the next morning.

That was the day I decided on my revenge.

(Lights come on as before.
Reema is still staring at the priest.
He is looking back at her, waiting.)

PRIEST: *(Watching her kindly)*

You shouldn't mind, child, if he didn't come to you. Sometimes, when we are in dire misery, we avoid those we love. In those situations we turn to strangers for solace.

REEMA: *(Thinks about it and then turns to Shanaz)*

He turned to you; he came to you that night. He came to you and you took him in and tended to him. *You* met him that night.

SHANAZ: *(Looking down, in a low voice)*

Yes, he came to me, *I* met him that night. But there was nowhere to take him *in*. We were both on the run.

(Looks up straight at Reema.)

I found a place, a hole in a wall, and hid him. I tended to him. I wasn't going to let a wounded Muslim die on the street.

(Painfully remembering)

They had come at us with everything they could use: sticks and swords and guns and tridents. They shot at us, they threw knives at us, they butchered us. There was nowhere to run then also but some of us escaped by playing dead. They left us for dead and then they went back to their lives laughing at our plight, eating the same dal-roti, enjoying the same TV programmes – whatever they had interrupted for a moment.

(Silence for a moment.)

PRIEST: *(To Shanaz)* .

You shouldn't let your acrimony ruin your life because of what they did to you, child. Let us not spend our time on earth in hatred because of some black sheep like those outside there right now. Revenge belongs to me, says our Lord. We have to learn to forgive.

SHANAZ: *(To the priest, defiantly)*

Forgiveness can also be seen as a weakness by the perpetrator, Father. As a license to commit the same atrocities over and over, again and again. Only the strong and the powerful can afford the luxury of forgiveness.

PRIEST: No, child. Violence only breeds further violence. Somewhere there has to be an end to it. And withholding forgiveness is also violence, child.

REEMA: And your not giving any succour to a wounded man, turning him away from the Lord's door, was that not a kind of violence too, violating humanitarian principles of your creed?

PRIEST: *(Looking straight ahead)*

That night has weighed heavy on me. I have tried to delve into my own mind and also into this tendency to violence since that night. I have tried hard. But I have not found any of the Lord's words to guide me. That night still weighs heavy on me.
I pray. I pray all the time but what He does with our prayers, our pleas and our expectations is as per His design. If He denies them to us, then we have to look within ourselves. If we don't receive His grace, then the fault lies with us.

(Lights dim on stage.

Only one light focuses on the priest.
The priest bows his head.
The priest's voice-over is heard in background.)

PRIEST'S
VOICE-OVER: That night still weighs heavy on me. I have
prayed and prayed but I have not received
the Lord's grace.

(Looks upward)

Oh Lord, I know the fault lies with me. My
faith has not been as strong as I thought it
to be. My mind is still troubled. Help me get
over my weakness, Lord!

(In a tormented voice)

My Lord has forsaken me.

(Hangs his head in abject mortification.)

I am not worthy of the Lord's grace. I am not
fit to guide my flock anymore.

I have to withdraw from this world; I have to
find a monastery and spend my remaining
years in praying for the absolution for
my transgression.

(Pause)

But right now, here and at this moment, my
Lord has still imposed a duty on me. Duty
of spreading the Lord's message. Duty of
praying for the misguided ones, duty of
seeking the Lord's grace for them. Right now,
I still have my obligations to fulfil.

(Lights come on as before.
The priest straightens his shoulders and looks up.)

PRIEST :   My children, Jesus Christ gave one message

182

to this world and that is to love all; especially those who have strayed from the path. Like those who are out there brandishing their guns and knives right now. They are the ones most in need of our Lord's grace and our prayers.
So let us all pray for them my children, let us all pray for those misled ones who are outside there.

(Bows his head, closes his eyes and starts counting his rosary praying silently.
Reema watches him for a long moment and then gets up and stands looking down at him)

REEMA: No Father, prayers for them alone are not of any help anymore – if they ever were – because it is them outside there and it is them inside here too. Because we, all of us, harbour the germs of being them. There is no us and them, Father. It is all us.
So pray for us too if you will, Father, because then you will be praying for yourself also.

(The priest continues with his prayers without acknowledging her.
Reema backs away.)

REEMA: *(Looking away, speaking to herself)*

This night has changed something in all of us, hasn't it? It has broken a taboo; it has brought to surface all that had been kept hidden deep within us.

This night is not easy to live with. It is always easier to live with a pretence, always easier to play a game.

(Reema stands staring into the distance.
Lights on the stage fade out.
Only one light focuses on the clock.
In the silence the ticking of the clock becomes loud.
The clock shows midnight and starts tolling, each of its peals echoing ominously like a death knell.
Pause
Lights brighten on the stage
Shanaz has stood up.
All except the priest are standing frozen staring at the clock.
Long pause
Loud blasts and gunfire are heard closer now and red flashes light up the windows.
Everybody comes out of the stupor and stares at the windows in panic.)

MATHEW:
(Almost in tears)

Why us? Why us?

REEMA:
Because we are the ones who don't believe in this mindless violence, didn't start it, didn't ask for it, and didn't join it.
(Laughs harshly)
Ours, of course, is the calculated, meditated, perfectly directed violence. And therefore, Mathew, that makes us perfect targets of *this* violence.

(Still laughing harshly)
Welcome to the crocodile country.

(Mathew looks at her perplexed.
Salim quickly moves over to her, holds her
arm and leads her to the window and keeps
holding her.
Reema rests her head on his shoulder.
The firing sounds have subsided but the red flashes
still continue to show in the windows.
Everybody mutely stares out of the windows.
Long pause
Then Reema lifts her head and looks at Salim.)

REEMA: Sing us a song, Salim, not a song of hope
              and not a song of love, not one of courage or
              bravery, not a sad one and not a happy one,
              but just a silly, stupid song.

              (Salim looks at her for a long moment, then smiles
              at her and holds her by both her arms and then
              sings looking into her eyes.)

SALIM: *(Singing)*

When the night turns red, red, red
And the moon glows black, black, black

(Salim's feet start dancing to the tune)

Then this little cuckoo bird jumps out to say
Dance
Dance and dance and dance all along.

(Salim has let go of Reema and is now dancing wildly.
Reema throws her head back and laughs a despairing laugh holding both his arms, then lets go of him and joins him in singing while dancing wildly by herself.)

For this whole wide world is going the cuckoo way
For this whole wide world is going the cuckoo way.

(Salim and Reema are dancing crazily by the window.
Mathew and Shanaz have been watching them shocked and wide-eyed.
Then Shanaz starts dancing wildly where she is.
Mathew turns to watch her for a moment with his mouth agape and eyes wide and then he also starts dancing frantically where he is.
The priest does not look up.
Subdued gunfire and sounds of blasts are heard and red flashes are seen outside again but they continue to sing and dance through it all with a careless abandon born of desperation.)

SALIM, REEMA,
MATHEW and
SHANAZ: *(Singing and dancing wildly)*

When the rainbows burrow deep, deep, deep
And pots of gold rise up, up, up
Then this little cuckoo bird jumps out to say
Dance
Dance and dance and dance all night long
For you are living in the cloud-cuckoo-land anyway

For you are living in the cloud-cuckoo-land anyway
For you are living in the cloud-cuckoo-land anyway.

(During the last line of the song sounds of blasts and gunfire outside increase until they become one continuous noise and drown out the singing and the red flashes increase until the windows are bathed in a constant red light.

All four are still dancing wildly, frenziedly.

Slowly lights on the stage fade away and they all are silhouetted against the constant red light in the windows frozen in their dance postures.

The red light seeps on the stage from all sides and fills it and engulfs everybody and everything on it.

The gunfire and grenade blasts outside become thundering.

Suddenly dead silence and total darkness envelop the stage.

Long pause

Loud ticking of the clock is heard in the darkness.

Pause

A faint glow shines on the clock.

The clock shows six am and tolls six times, its peals sounding very loud and echoing in the silence.

On the last peal the glow on the clock and its ticking fade away.

An eerie silence pervades the stage.

Pause

A pale dawn light creeps in through the windows and spreads around the stage.

Salim and Reema are standing at the window with their arms around each other and their backs to others.

Mathew is standing frozen against the wall, his mouth agape.

Shanaz is sitting rigid on a hard chair staring straight ahead with her mouth set.

The priest is sitting on the sofa counting his rosary, praying silently with his head bowed.

Long pause

The faint glow shines on Salim and Reema.

Salim turns and looks at Reema.

Reema turns and looks into his eyes without speaking.

Salim holds her eyes for a long moment, then, still wordlessly, turns his back on her and, in a slow motion, slips out through the rear door.

Reema turns back to the window.

Pause

The glow moves to shine on Shanaz.

Shanaz comes to life, looks at the priest, clamps her mouth and turns the corners of her mouth down.

After a long moment she turns to look at Mathew and wrinkles her nose and forehead in disgust and then turns to look towards the rear door.

Pause

Shanaz stands up in slow motion.)

SHANAZ: *(Calling, her voice reverberating as in a cavernous space)*

Salim, wait for me, Salim.

(Shanaz rushes out, also in slow motion, through the rear door.
Nobody looks at her.

Her calling voice can be heard getting fainter and fainter until it fades away.)

SHANAZ: Saliiim... Saliiim... Saliiiiiim... ...

(Pause
The glow shines on Reema and moves with her.
Reema stands looking out of the window for a long moment, then turns and in a slow motion walks to the sofa, collects her handbag and opening it, rummages in it. She finds her car keys and without a glance at either the priest or Mathew walks out through the left archway – all in a slow motion.
Sound of a car starting and moving away, slowly fading away.
Pause
The glow shines on Mathew.
Mathew, who has been standing frozen, unfreezes, goes to the priest in a very slow motion, kneels in front of him, clasps his hands and bows his head. The glow has moved with him to include the priest.)

MATHEW: *(With his voice choking with remorse)*

Bless me, Father, for I have sinned.

(The priest slowly lifts his head and looks at Mathew's bent head for a time and then, in a slow motion, stands up, raises his arms and throws his head back to look heavenwards.)

PRIEST: *(Wailing in anguish)*

Forgive us, our Father in heaven, for we know not what we do.

(The words 'we know not what we do' echo a couple of times and then slowly fade away while the light gets hazy and the priest and Mathew – maintaining their positions – become just vague shapes in the hazy light.)

THE END

About the Author

Lalita Das is the author of the novel *Dancing with Kali* set in Goa where foreigners frolic on the beaches without restraint and where, in Hindu villages just a few kilometres inland, repressive traditions still rule and a young girl yearns for freedom of choice.

Born in Mumbai, she studied architecture in Sir J J College of Architecture, Mumbai, Planning and Urban Design in A A School of Planning, London, and Regional Planning at MIT, Boston.

A number of her project papers and articles on diverse subjects—interdependence of architecture and social systems, architecture designed by women, life of the *adivasis*—have been published in Indian and international publications. She has presented papers on town planning in ancient India and on position of women in Hinduism at various international conferences held in London, Manchester, Cardiff, Toronto and Colombo.

She is a practising architect and lives in Mumbai.